the secret box

Barbara Lehman

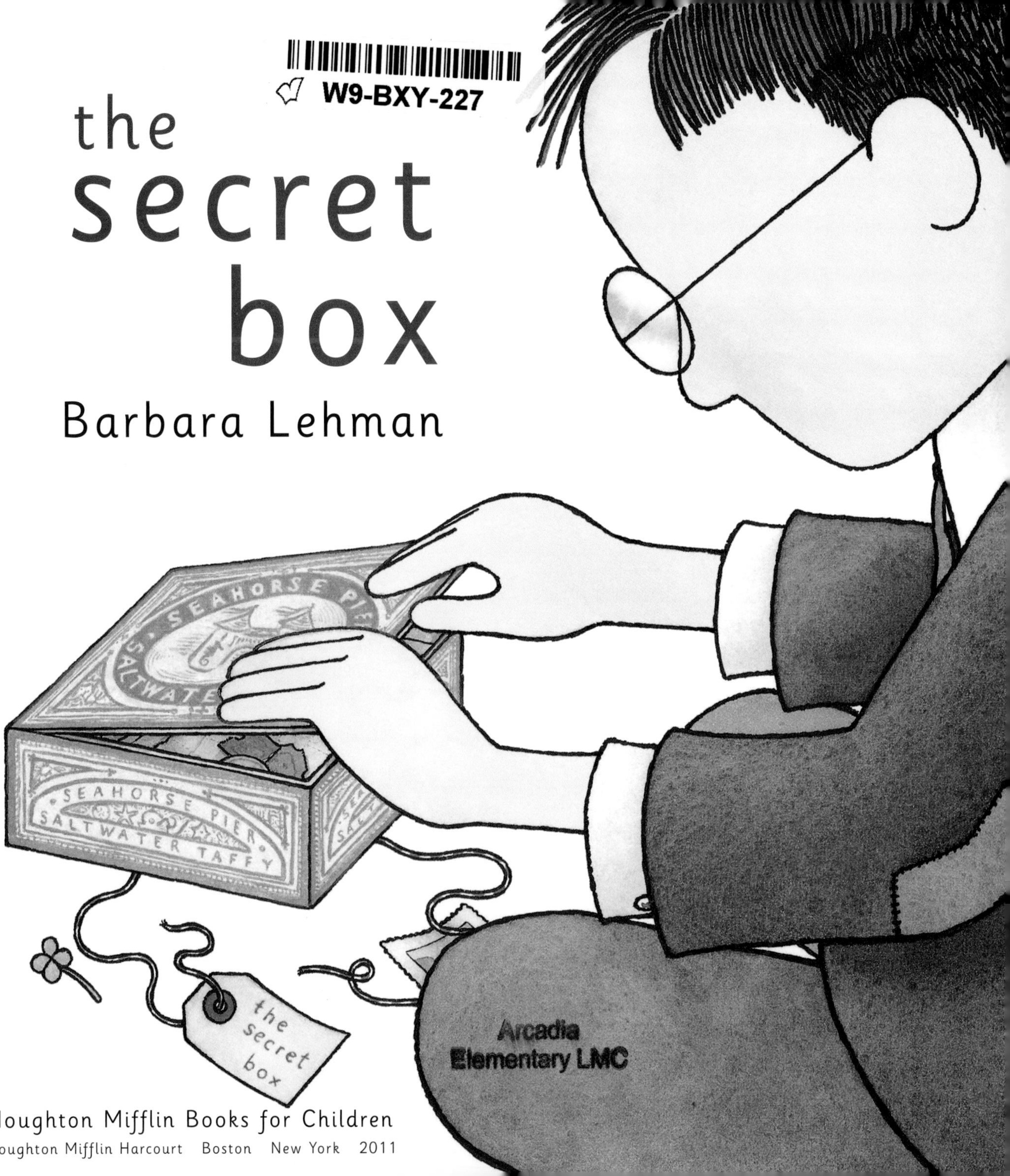
SEAHORSE PIER
SALTWATER TAFFY
SEAHORSE PIER
SALTWATER TAFFY
the
secret
box

Houghton Mifflin Books for Children
Houghton Mifflin Harcourt Boston New York 2011

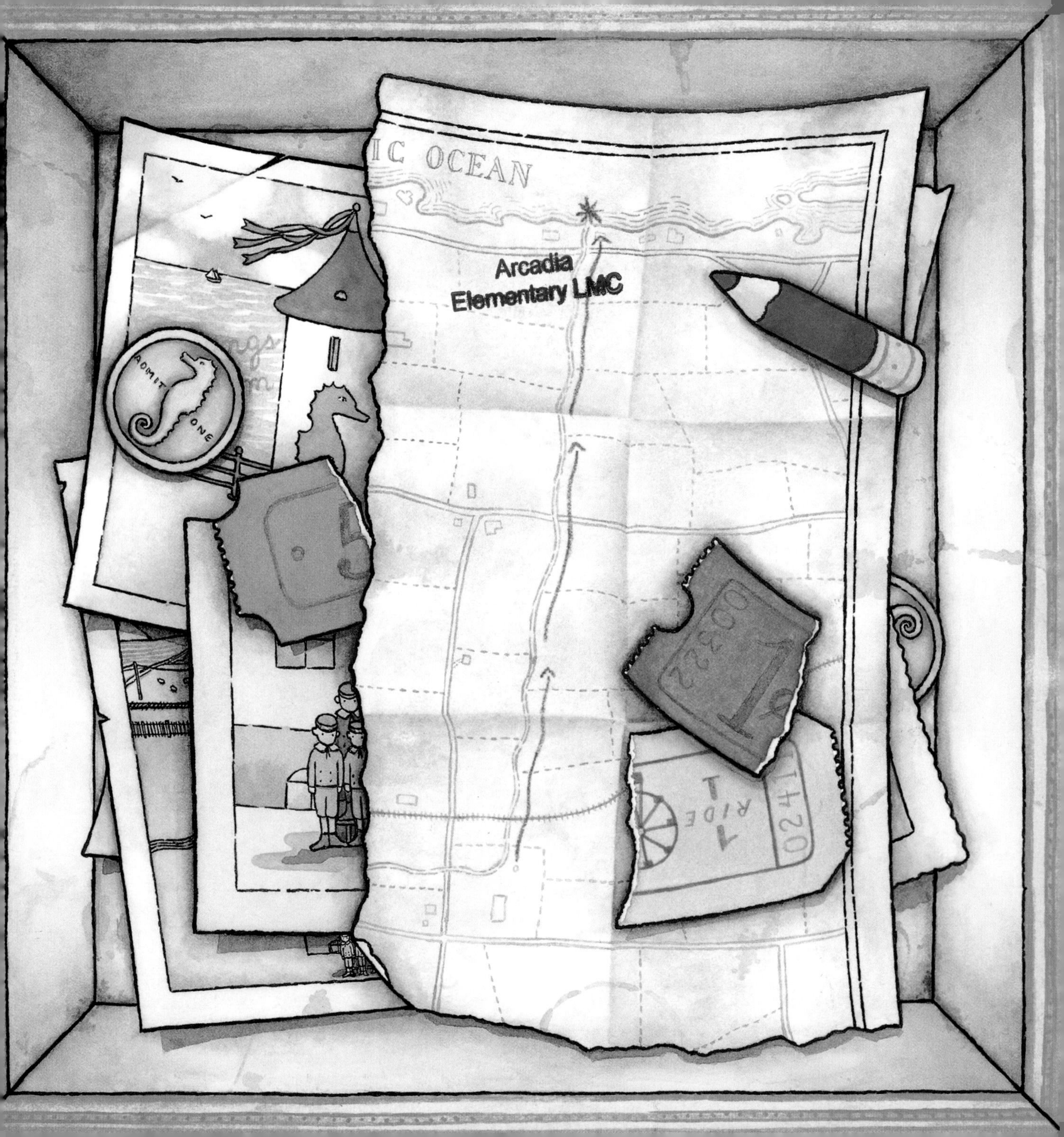
IC OCEAN
ADMIT ONE
RIDE

For Cee and Bill Boswell

Houghton Mifflin Books for Children is an imprint of Houghton
Mifflin Harcourt Publishing Company.

www.hmhbooks.com

The illustrations are watercolor, gouache, and ink.

Library of Congress Cataloging-in-Publication Data is on file.

ISBN 978-0-547-23868-5

Manufactured in Singapore
TWP 10 9 8 7 6 5 4 3 2 1
4500270347

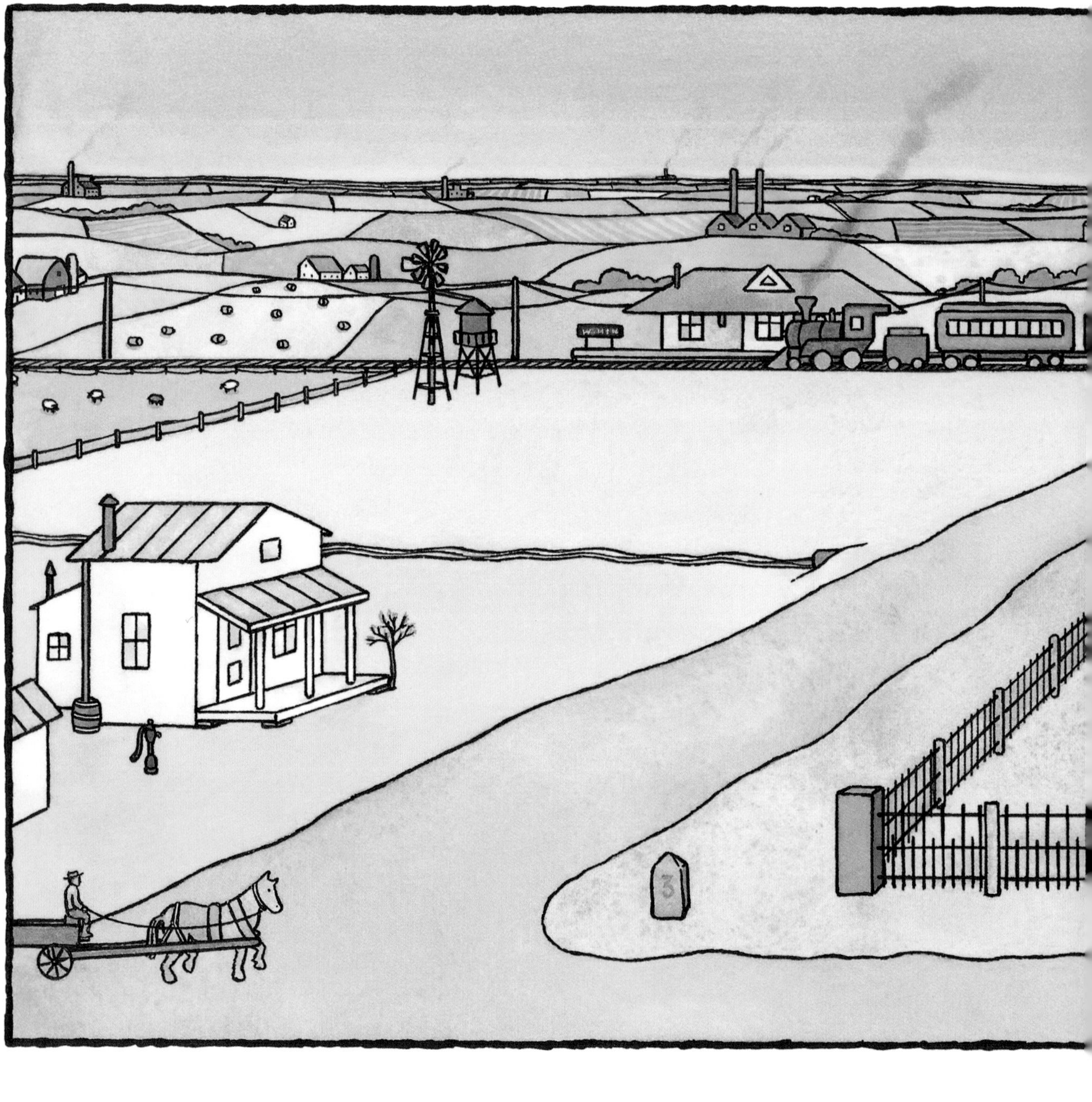
3

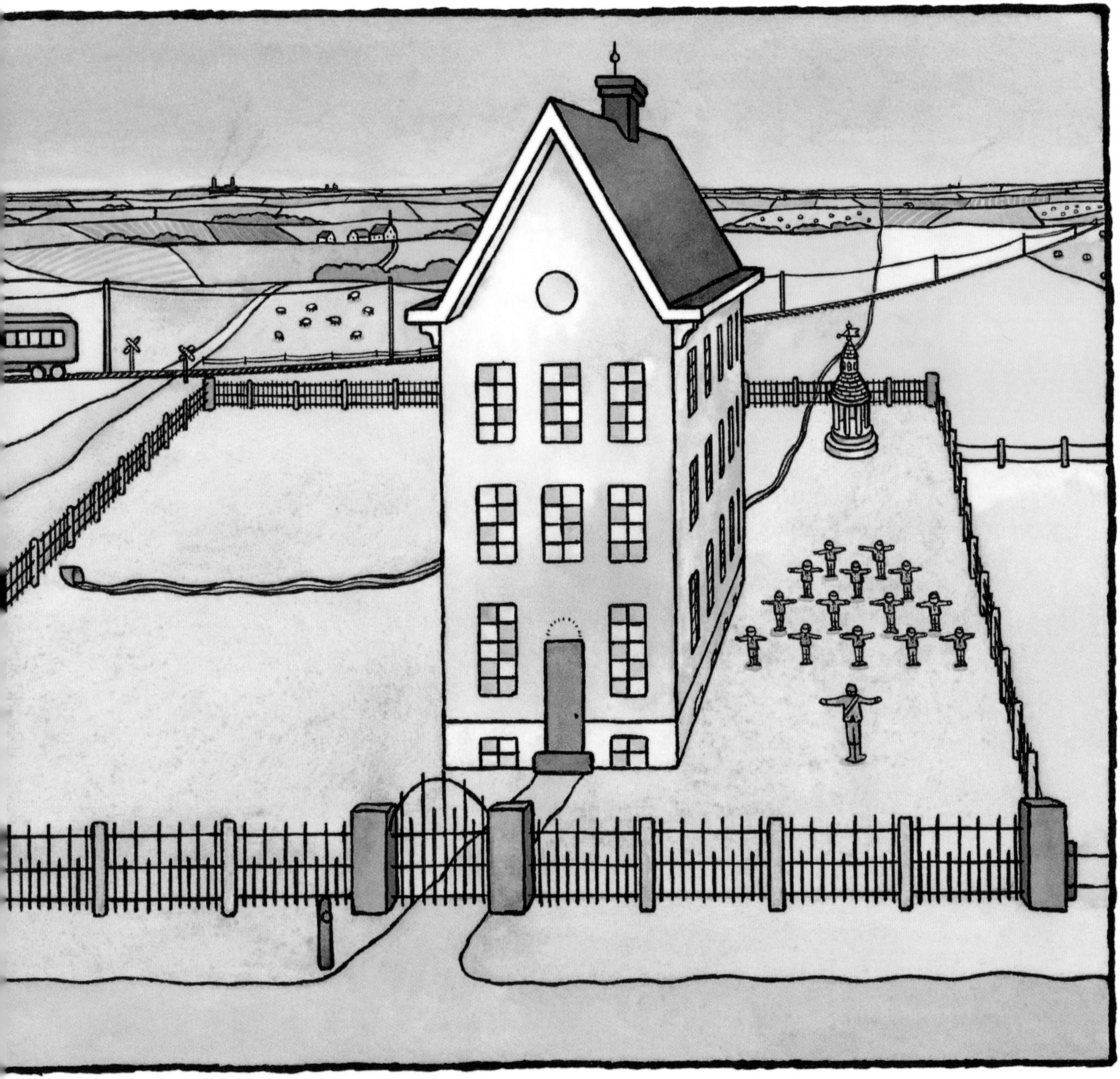

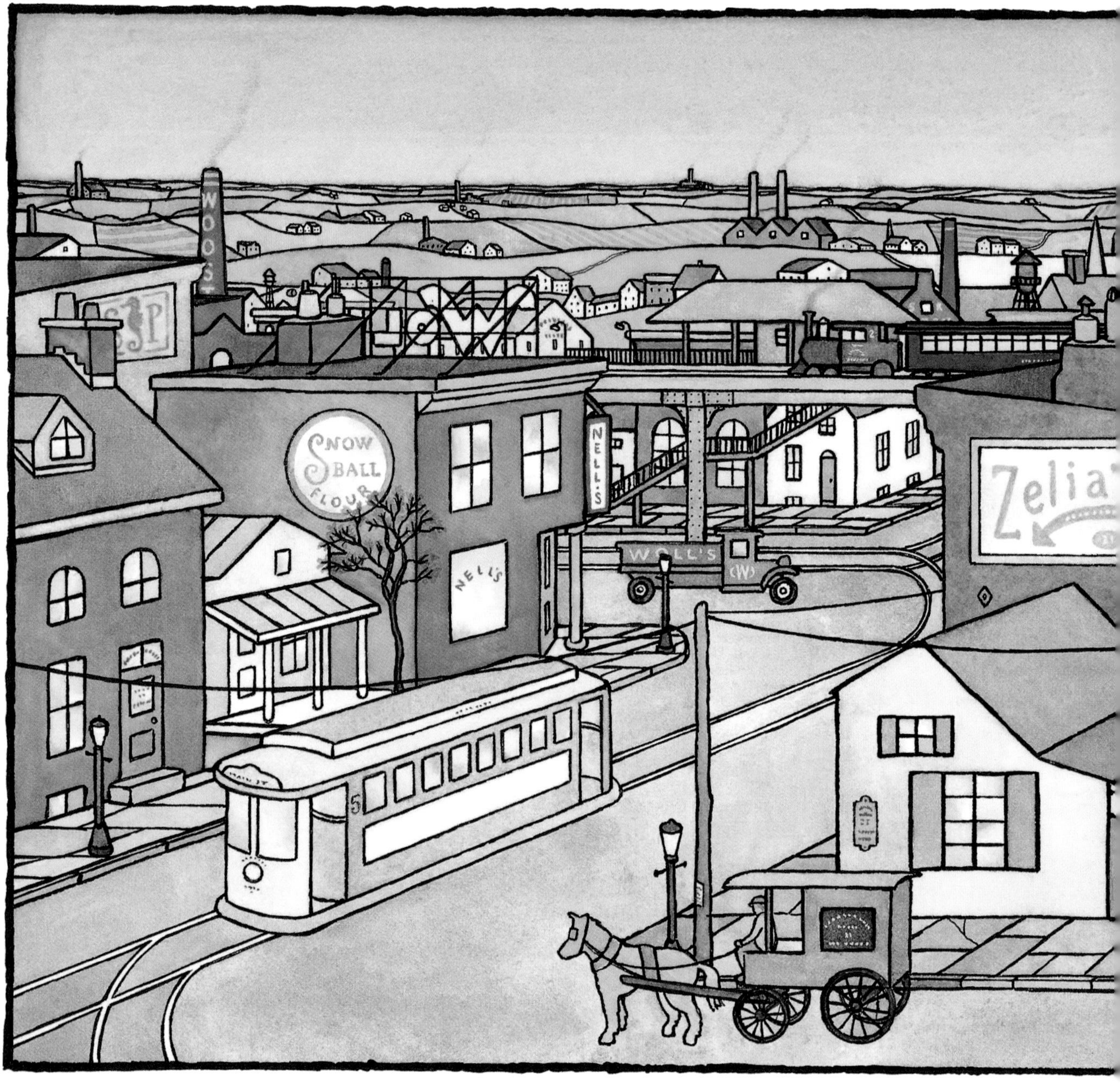
WOOST
SNOW BALL FLOUR
NELL'S
NELL'S
WOLL'S
5

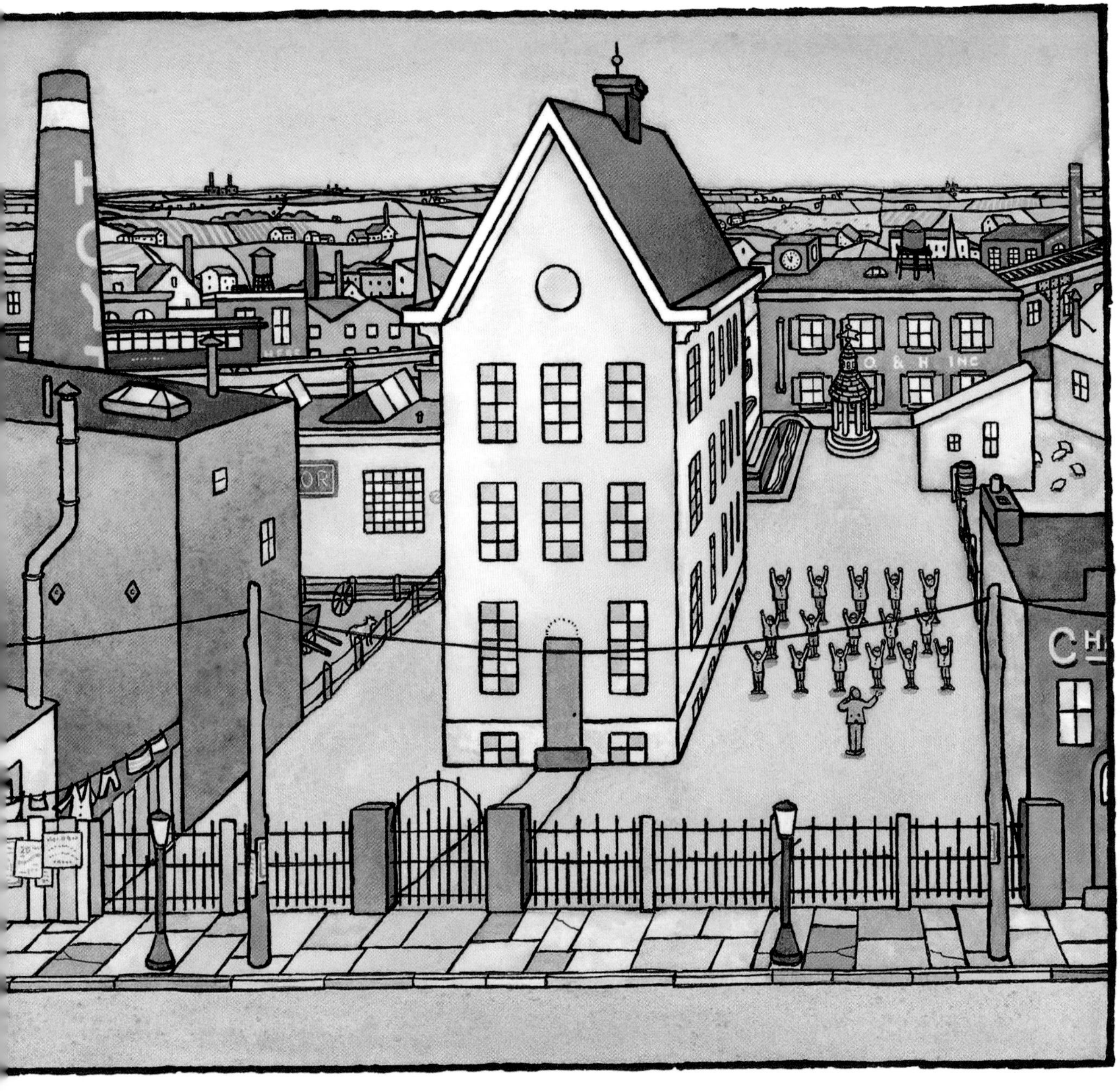
O. & H INC

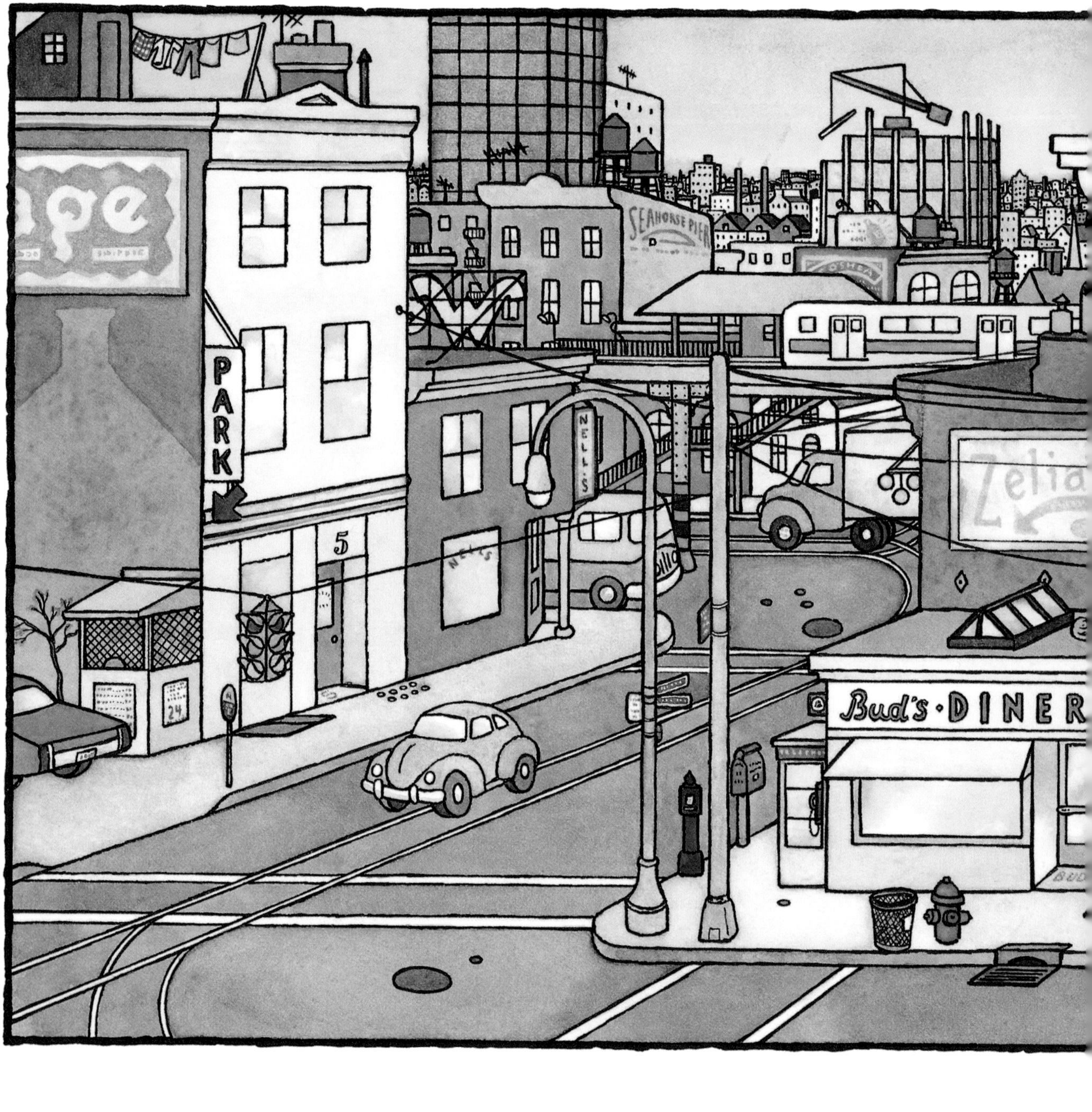
PARK
5
NELL'S
SEAHORSE PIER
24
Bud's · DINER

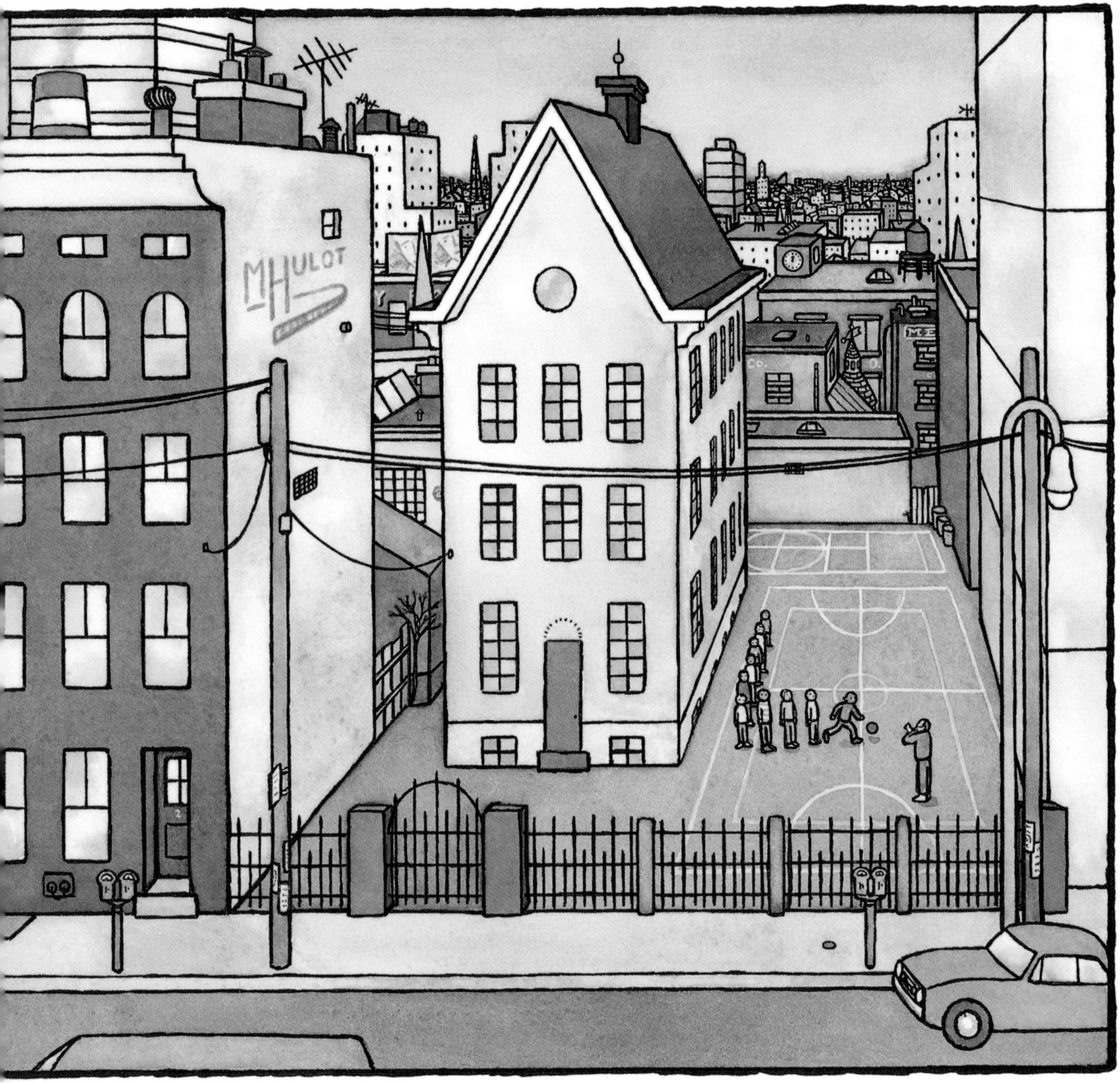
M HULOT

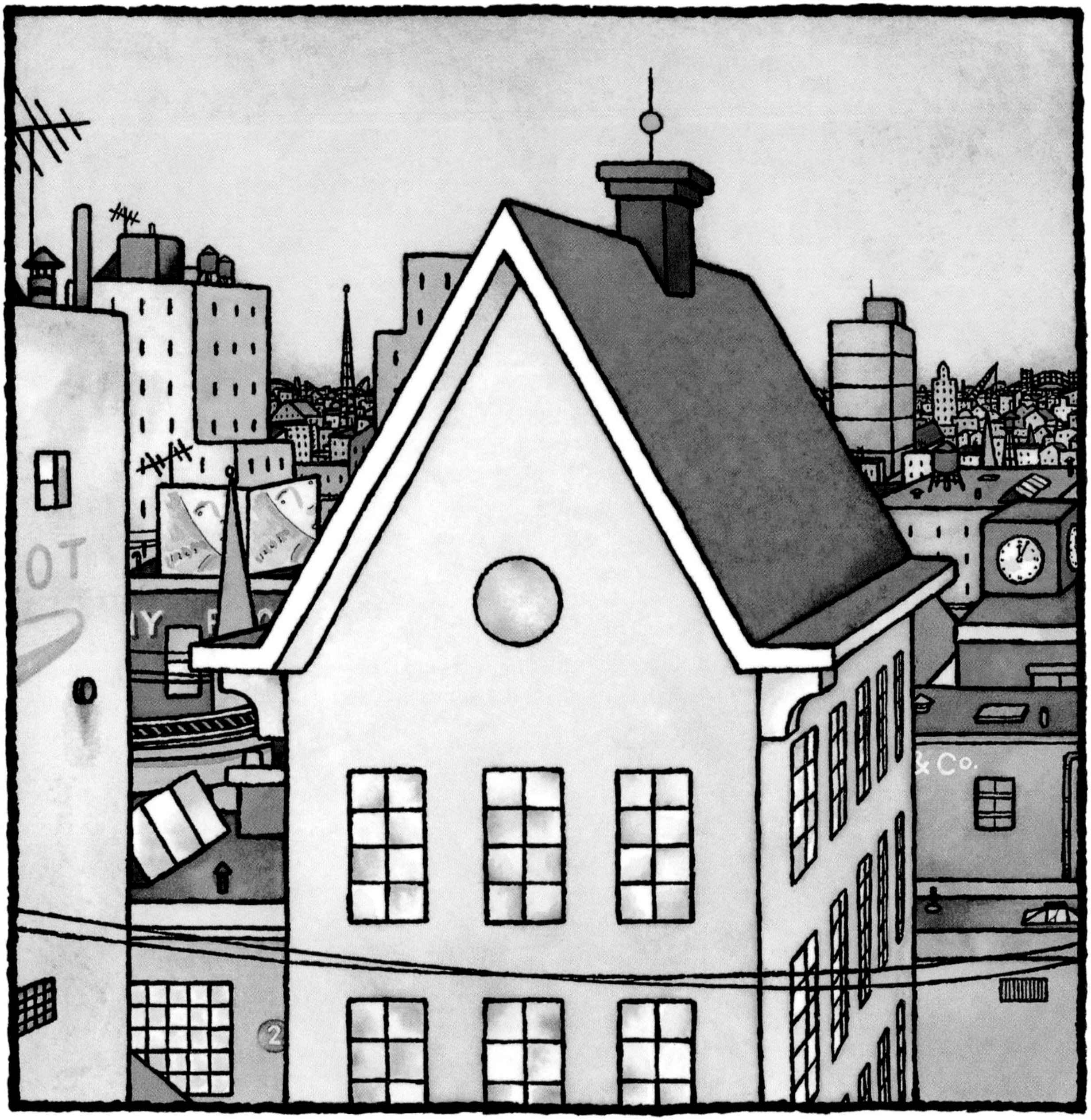

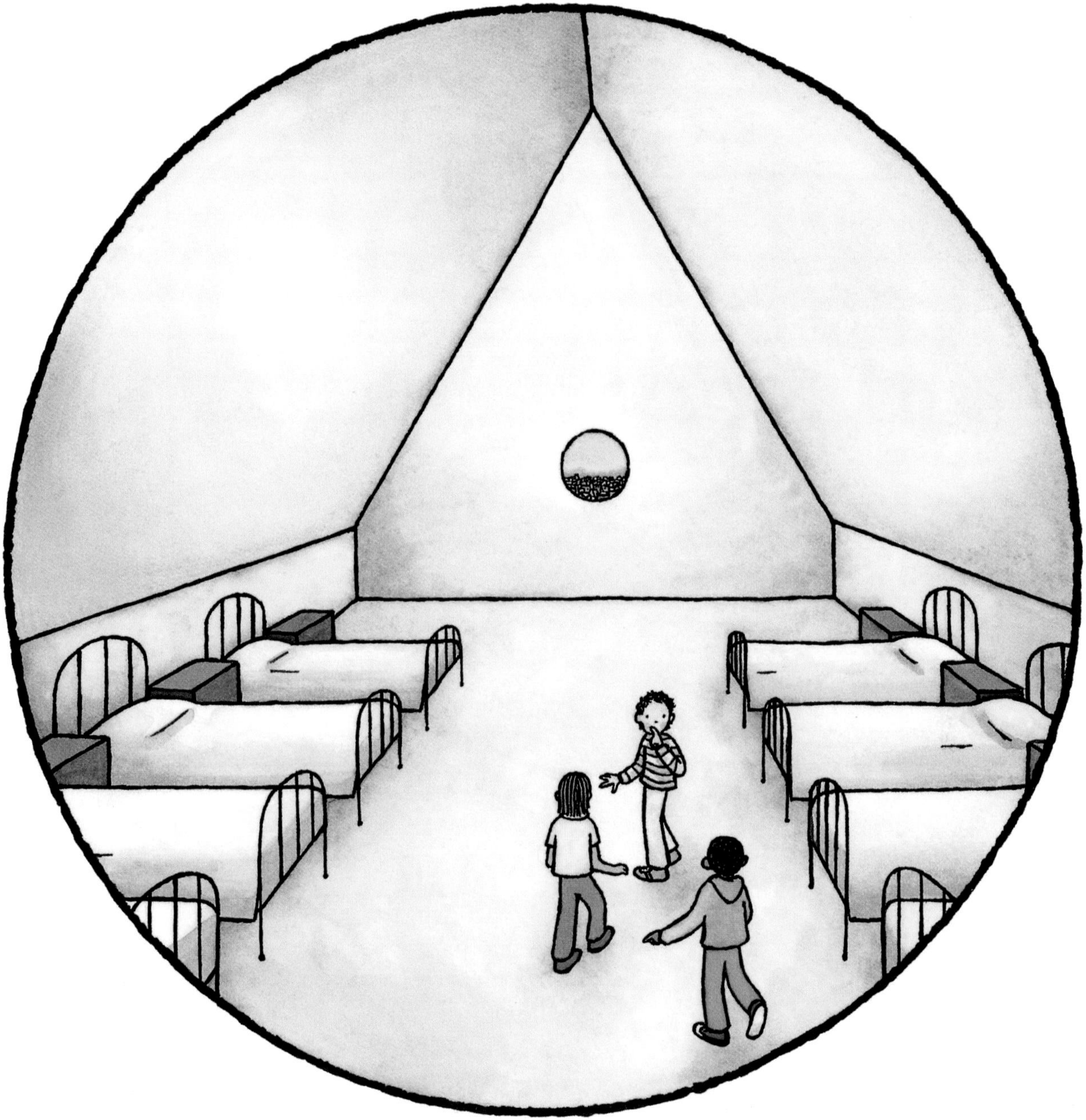

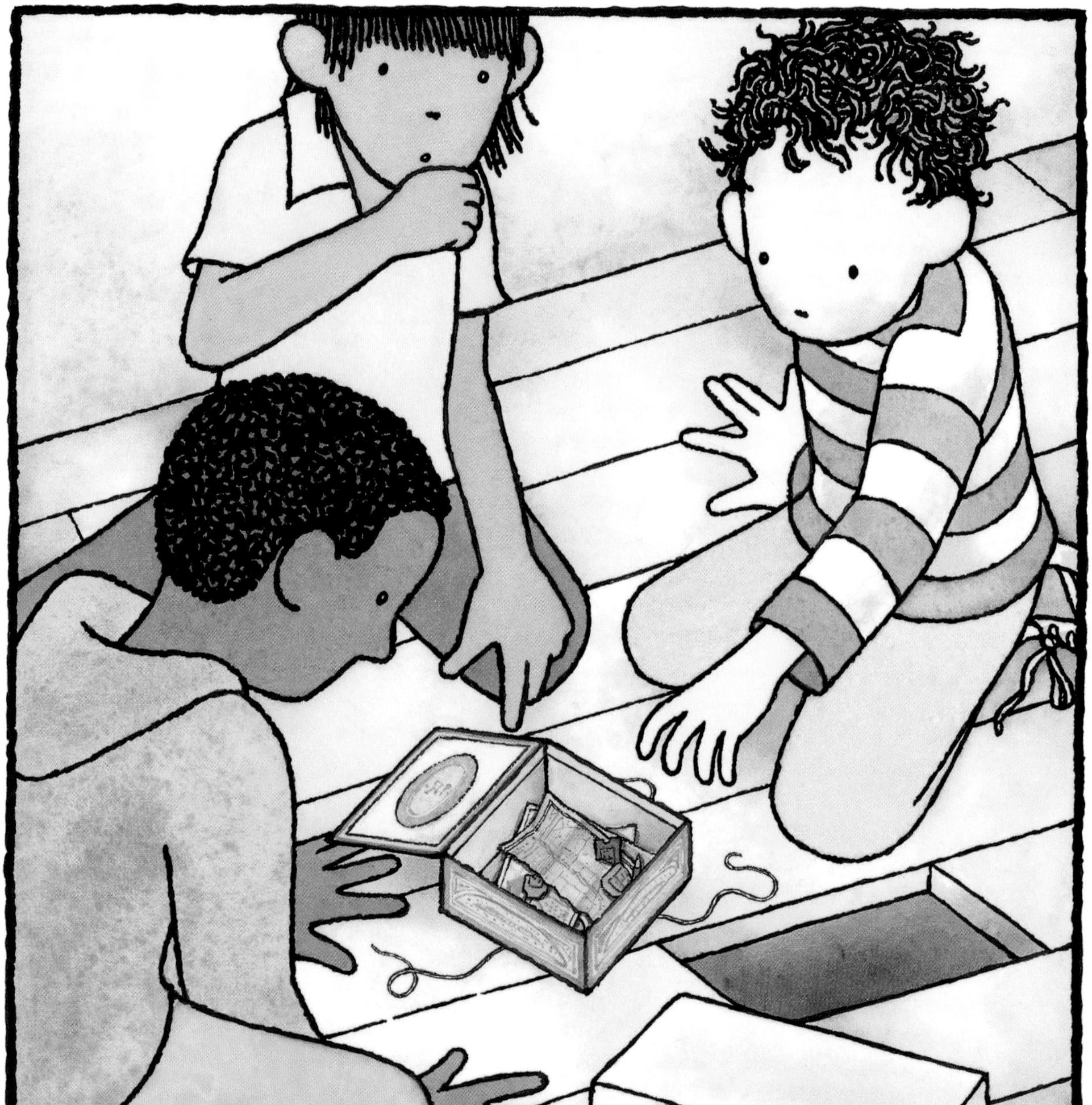

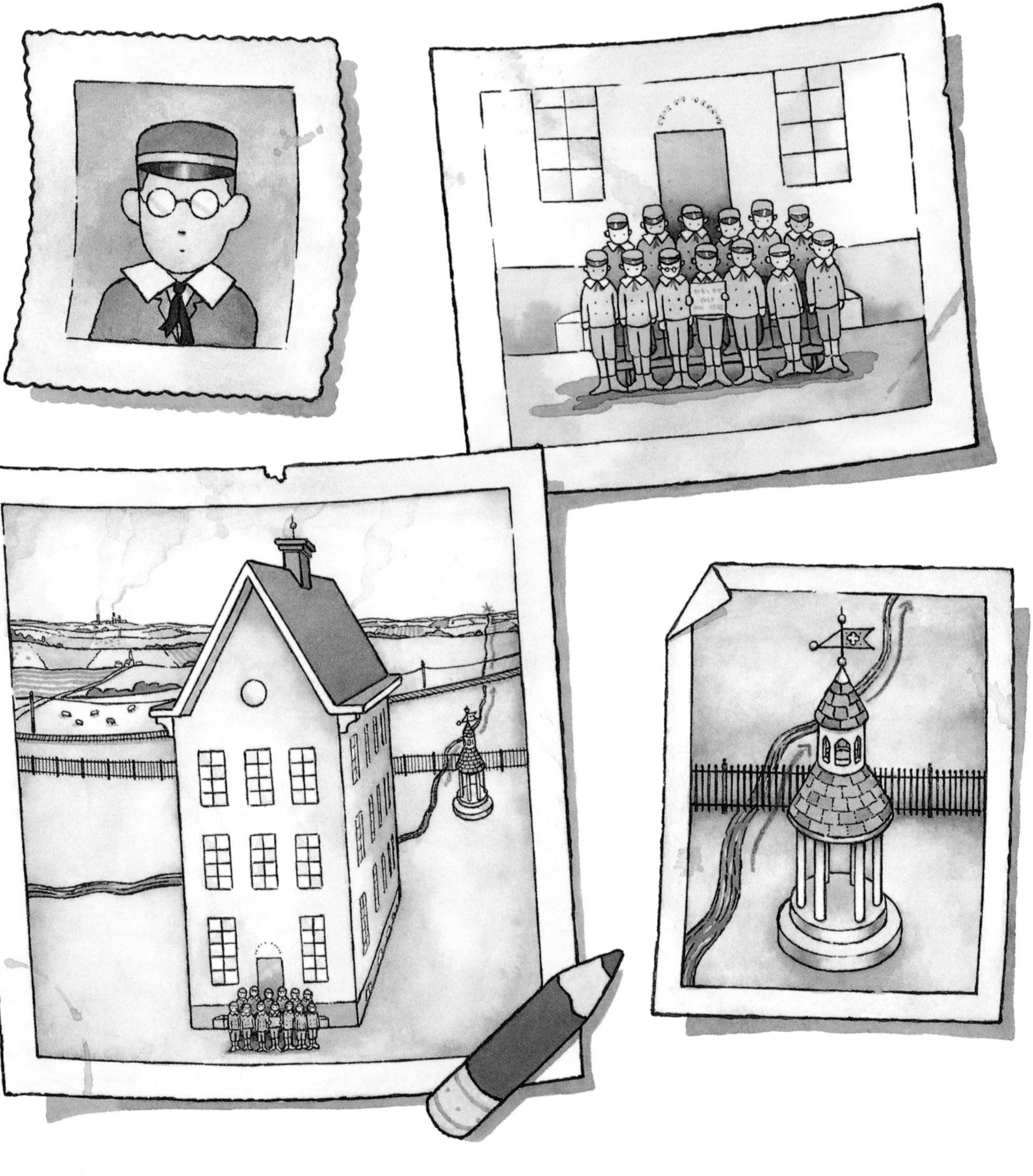

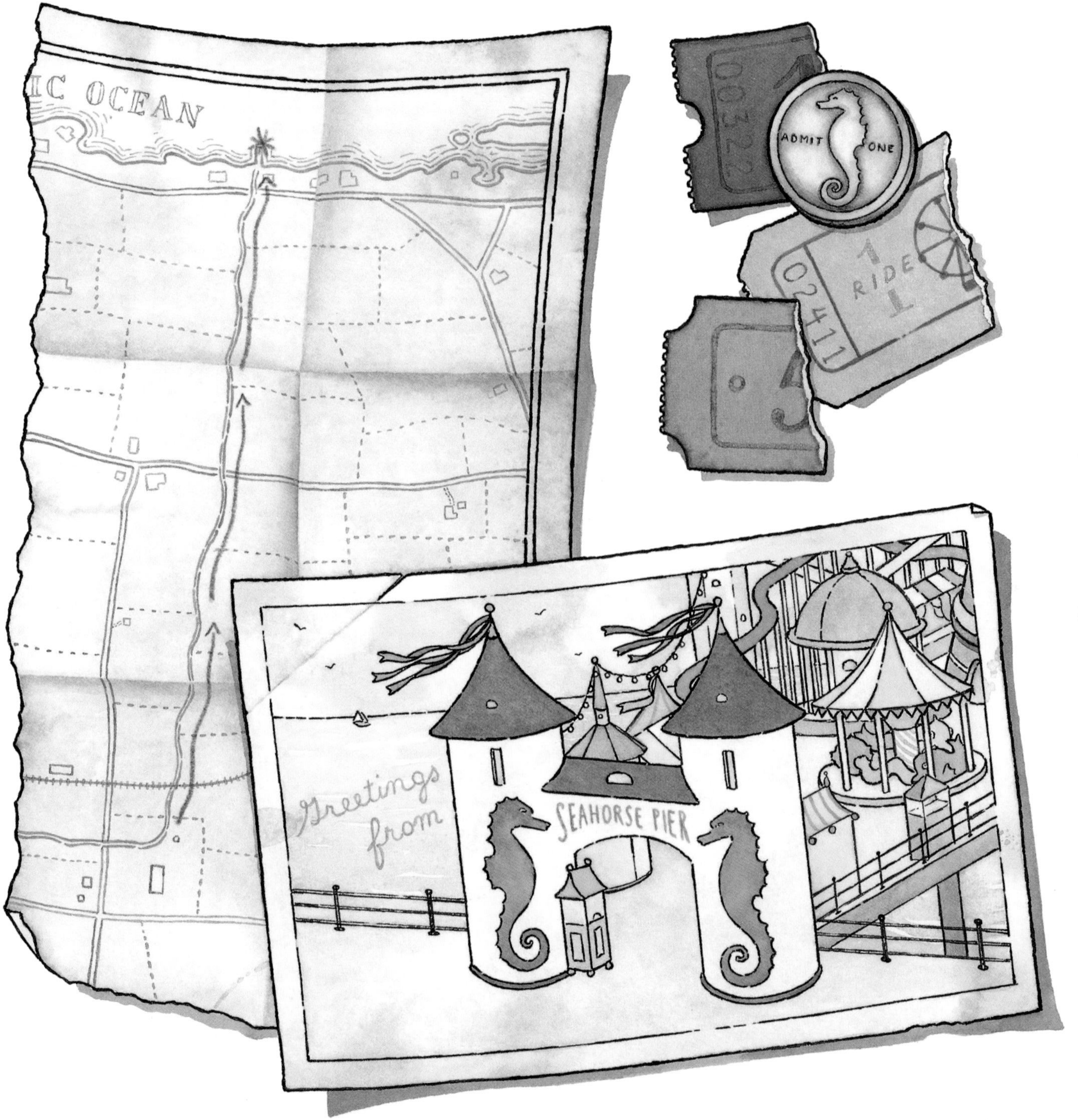
IC OCEAN
00322
ADMIT ONE
1 RIDE 1
02411
Greetings from
SEAHORSE PIER

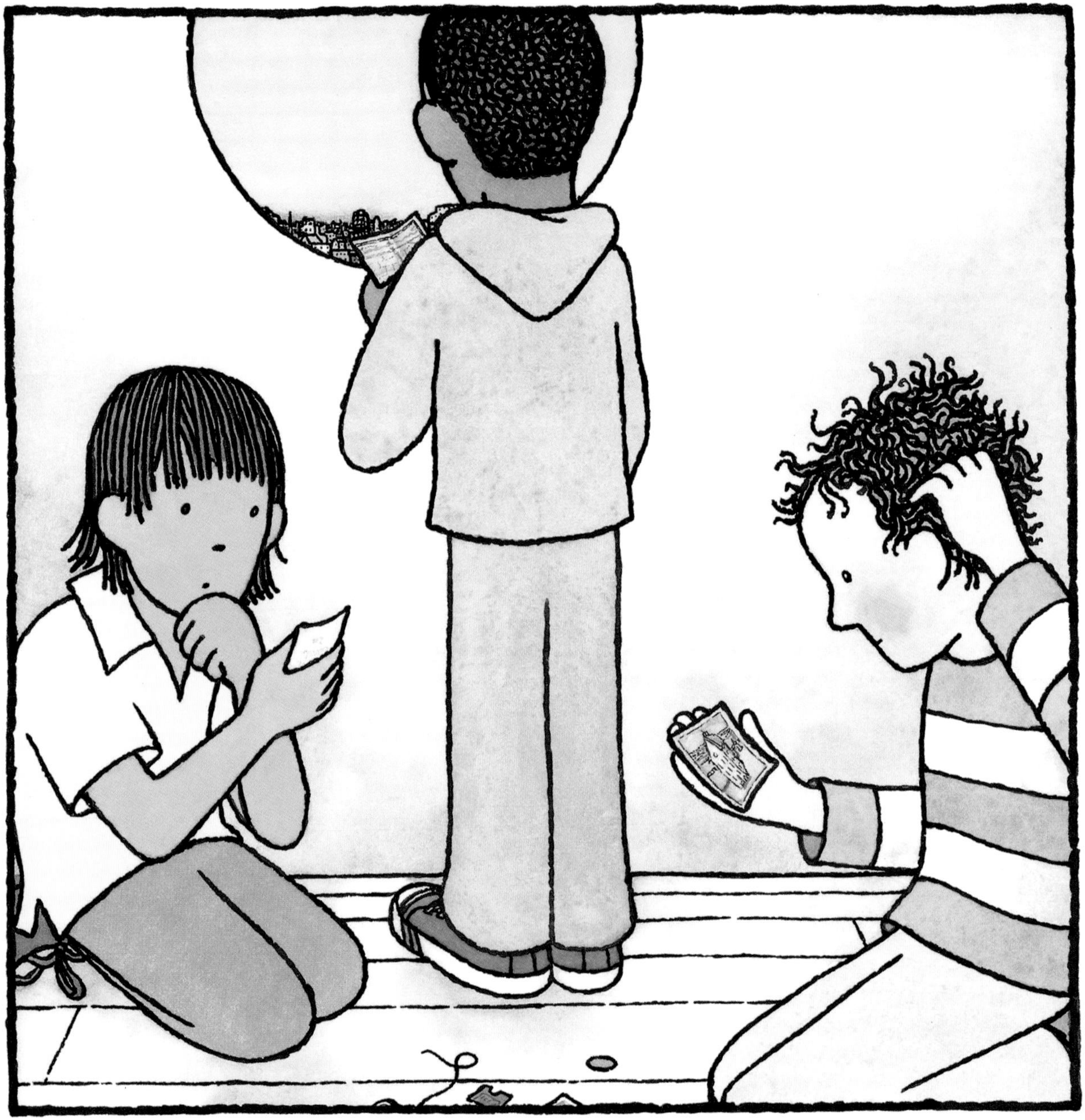

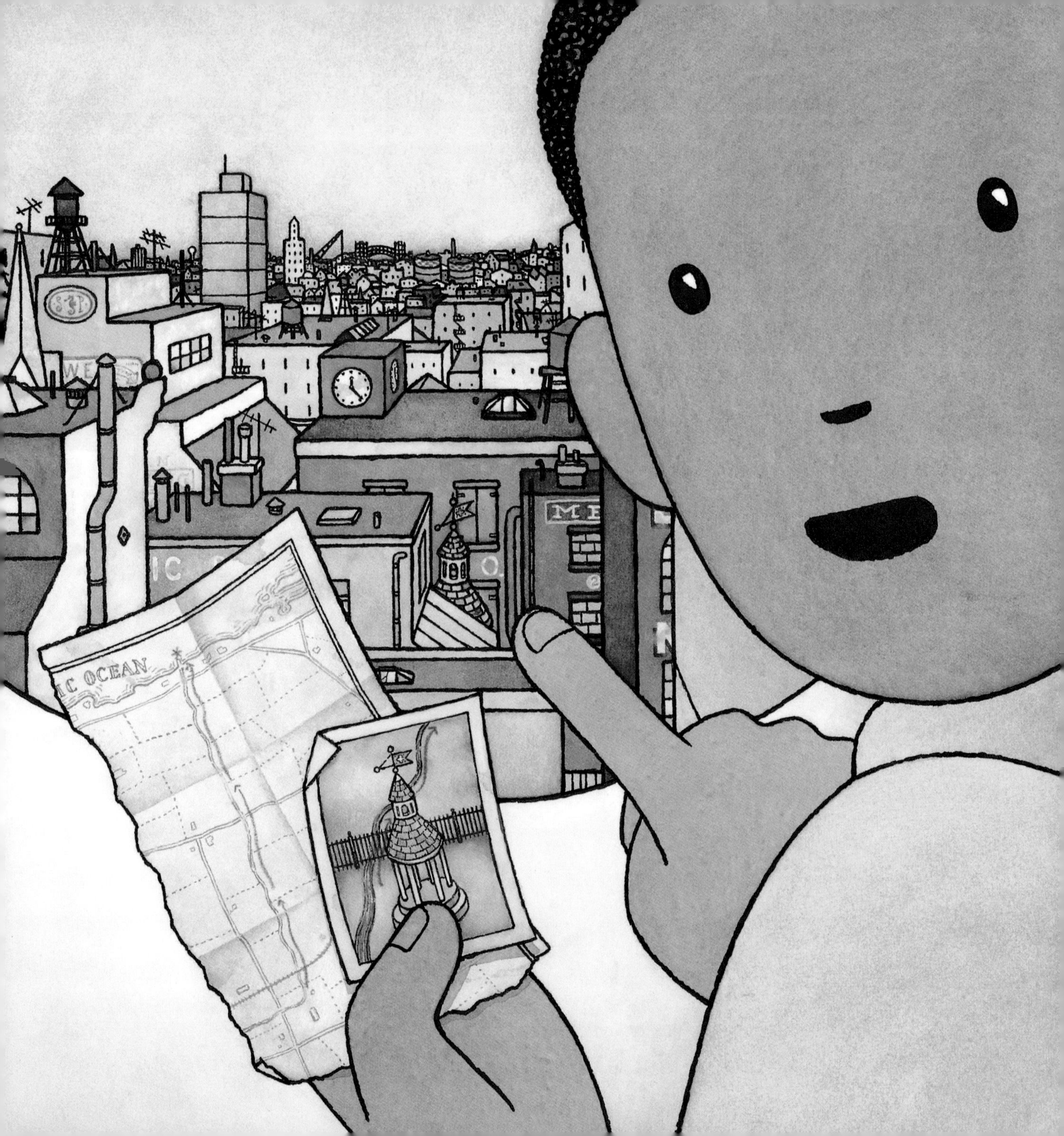
IC OCEAN

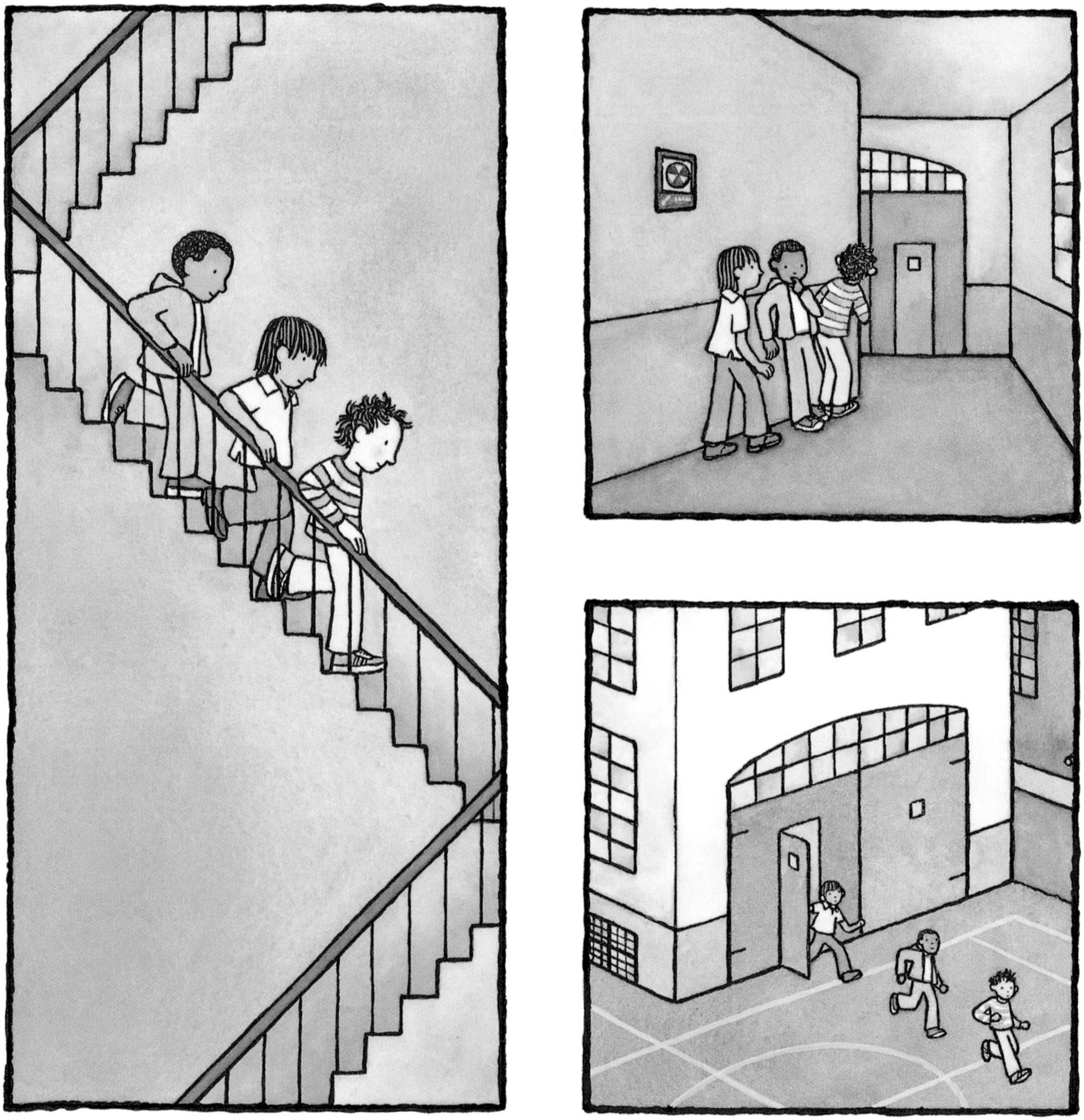

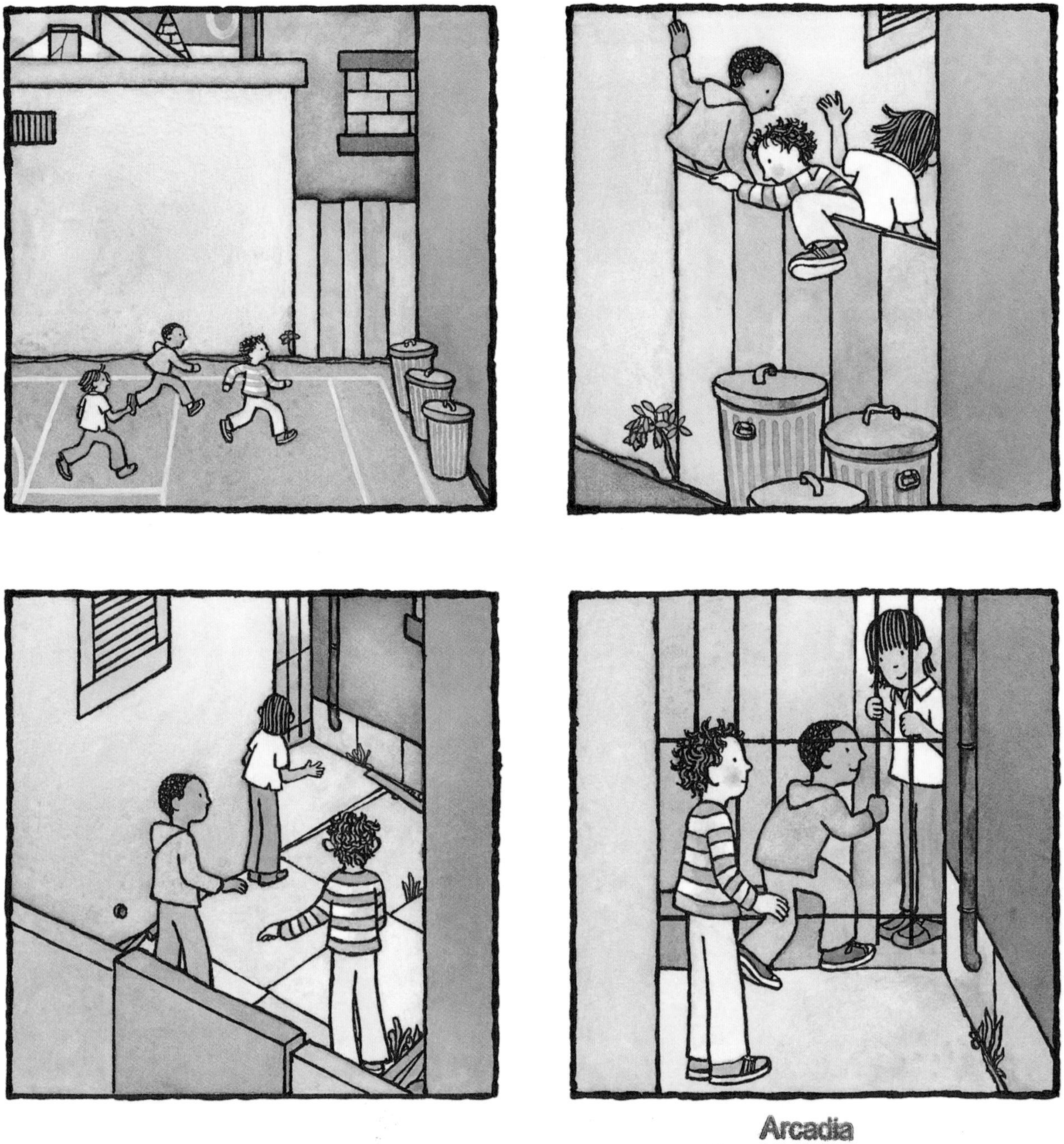

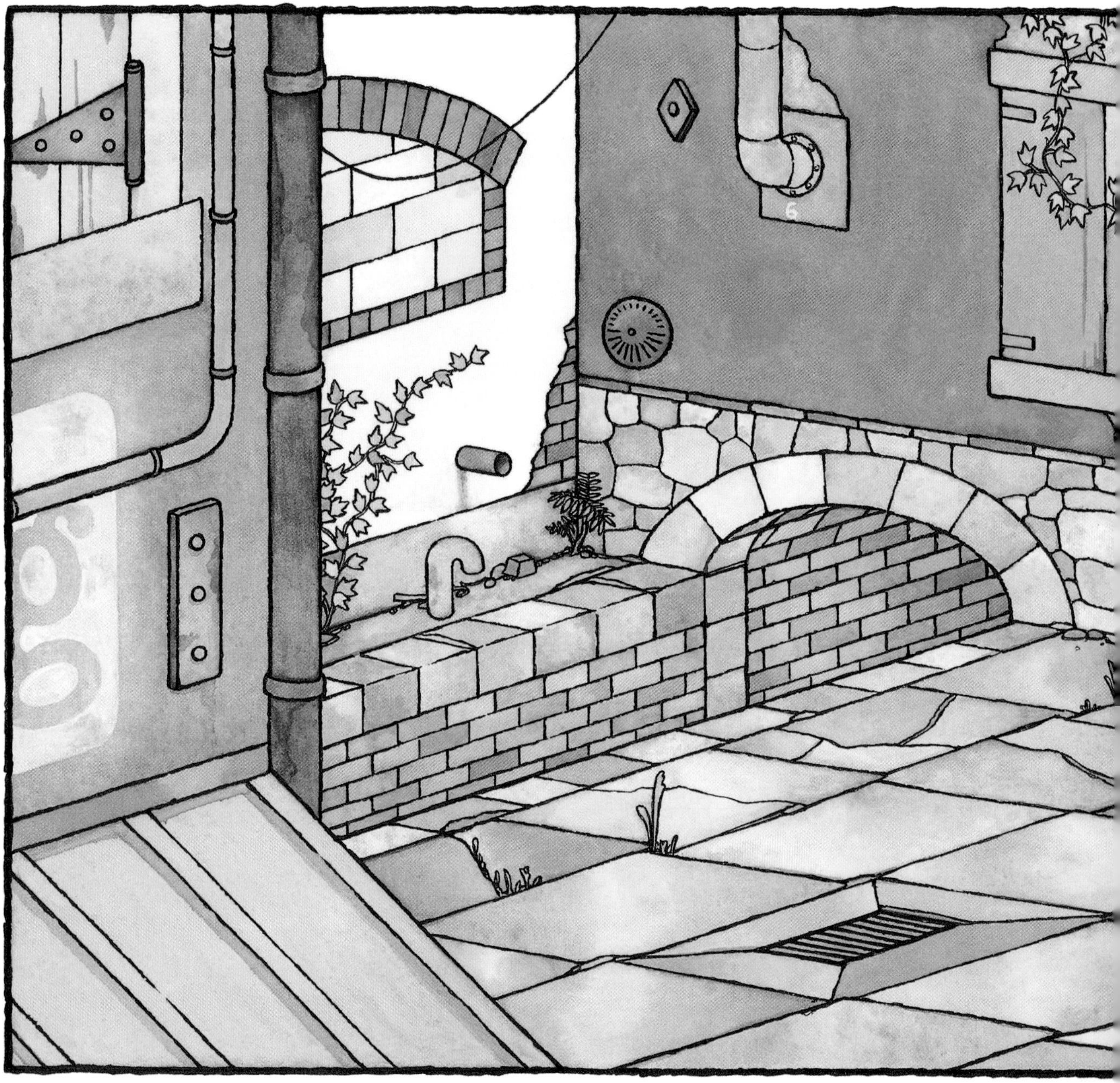
6

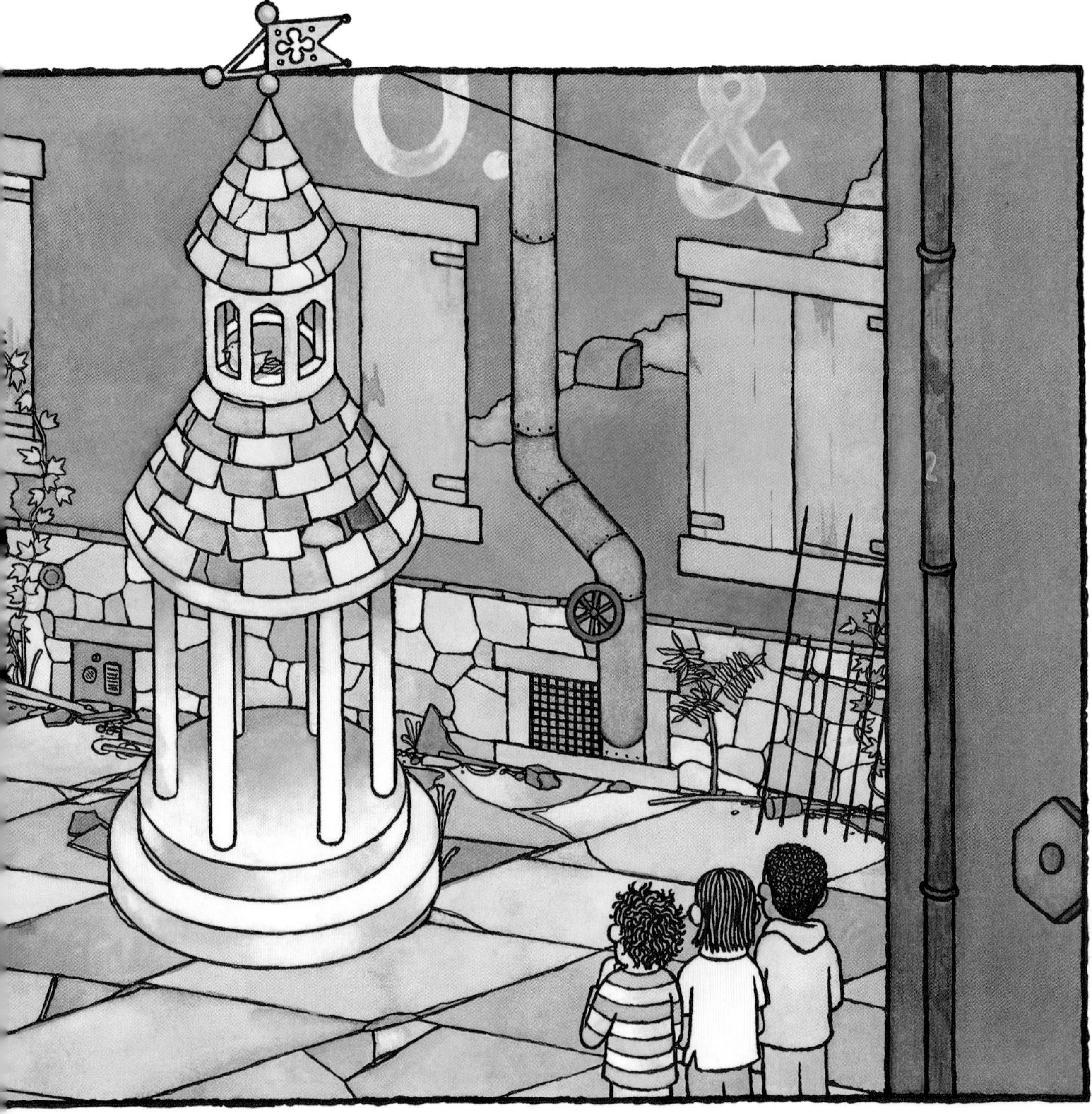

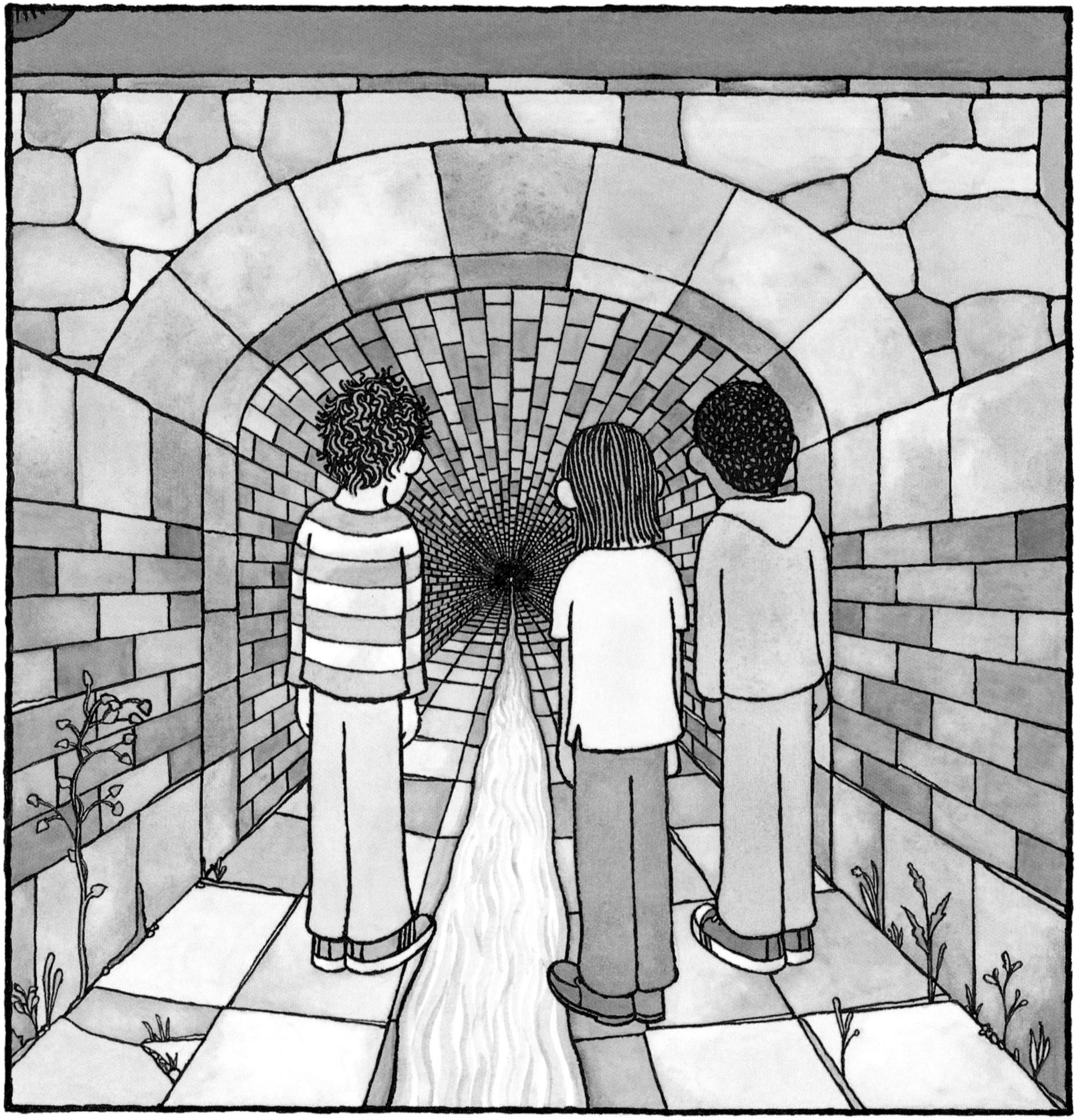

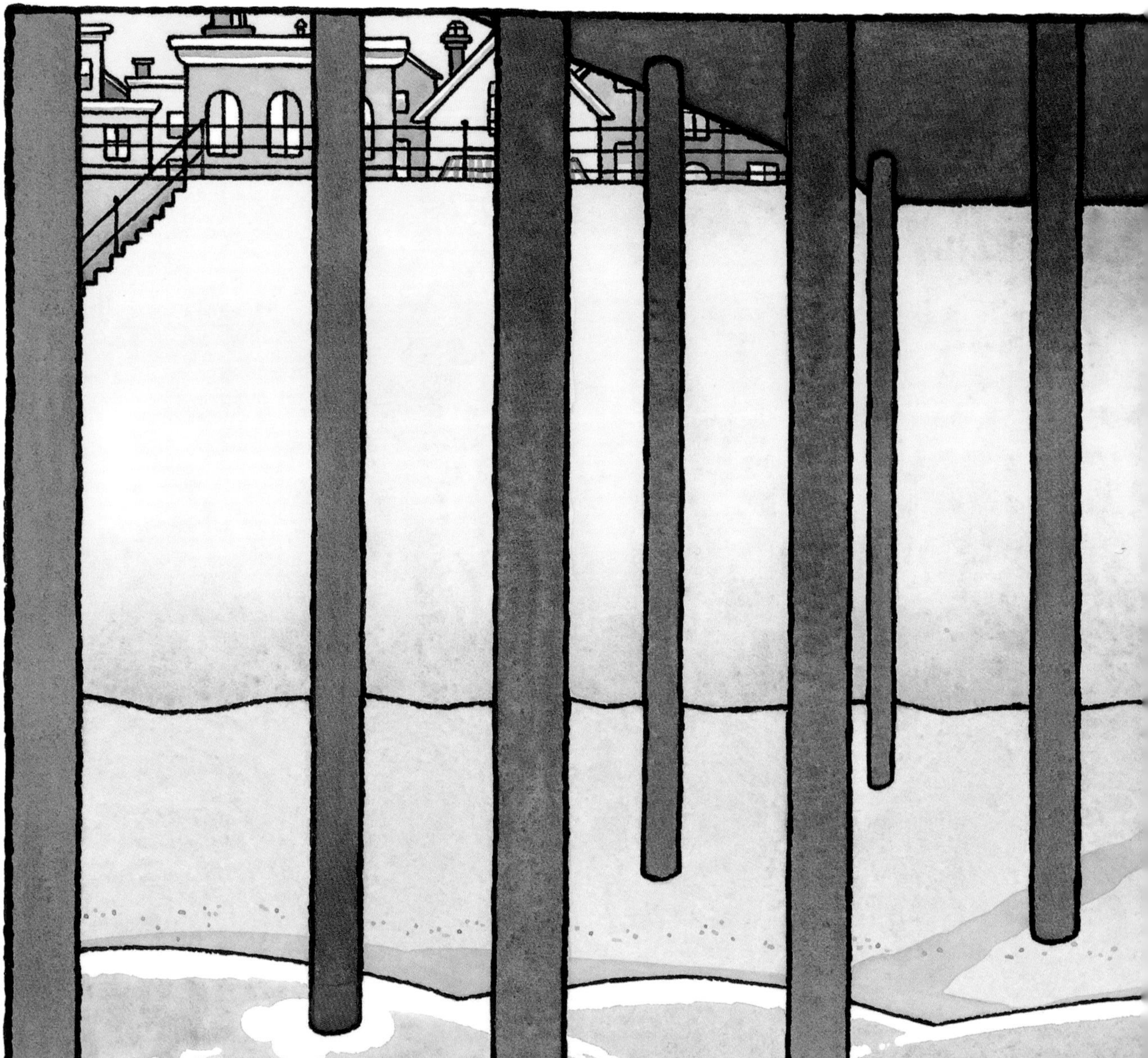

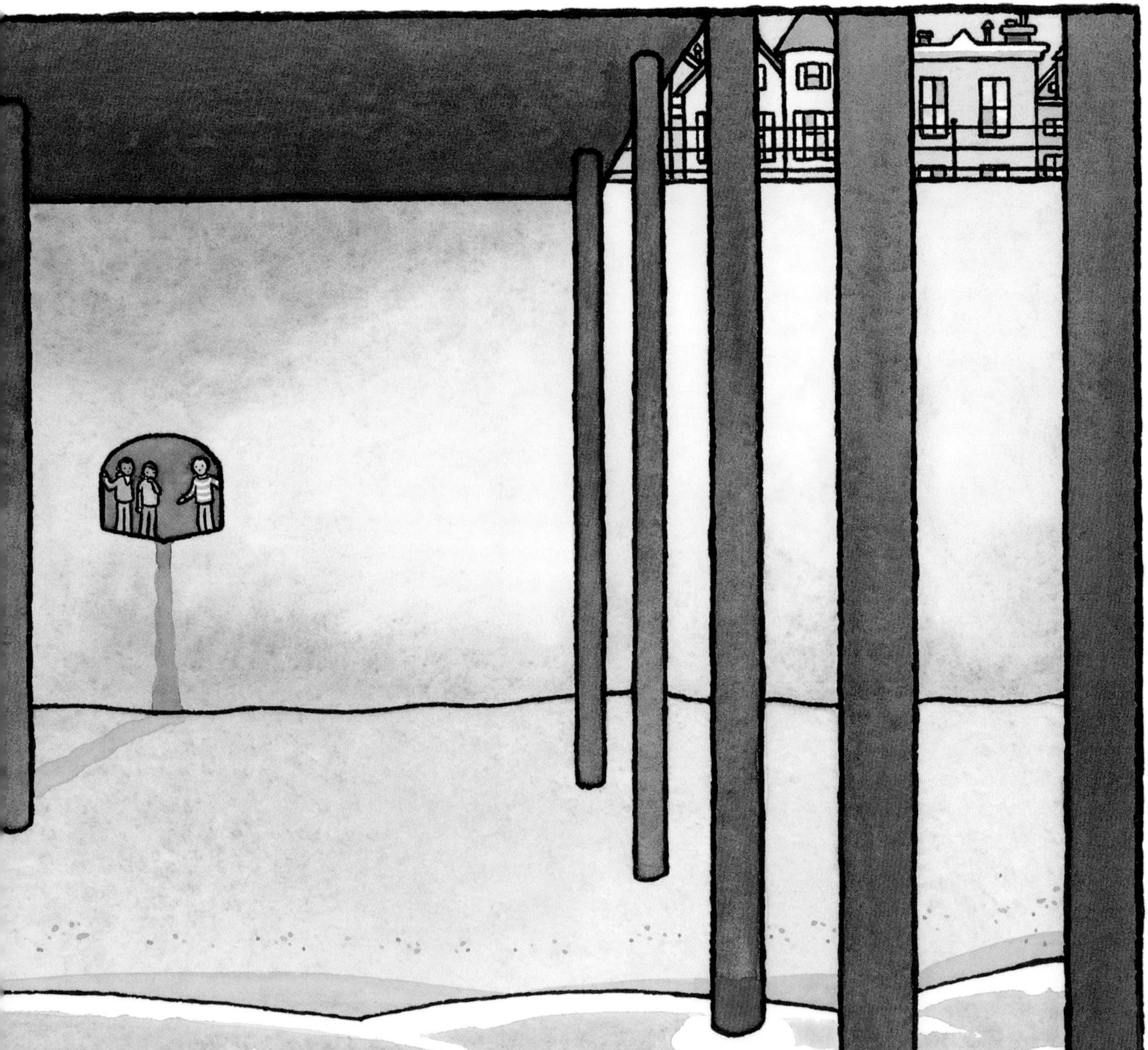

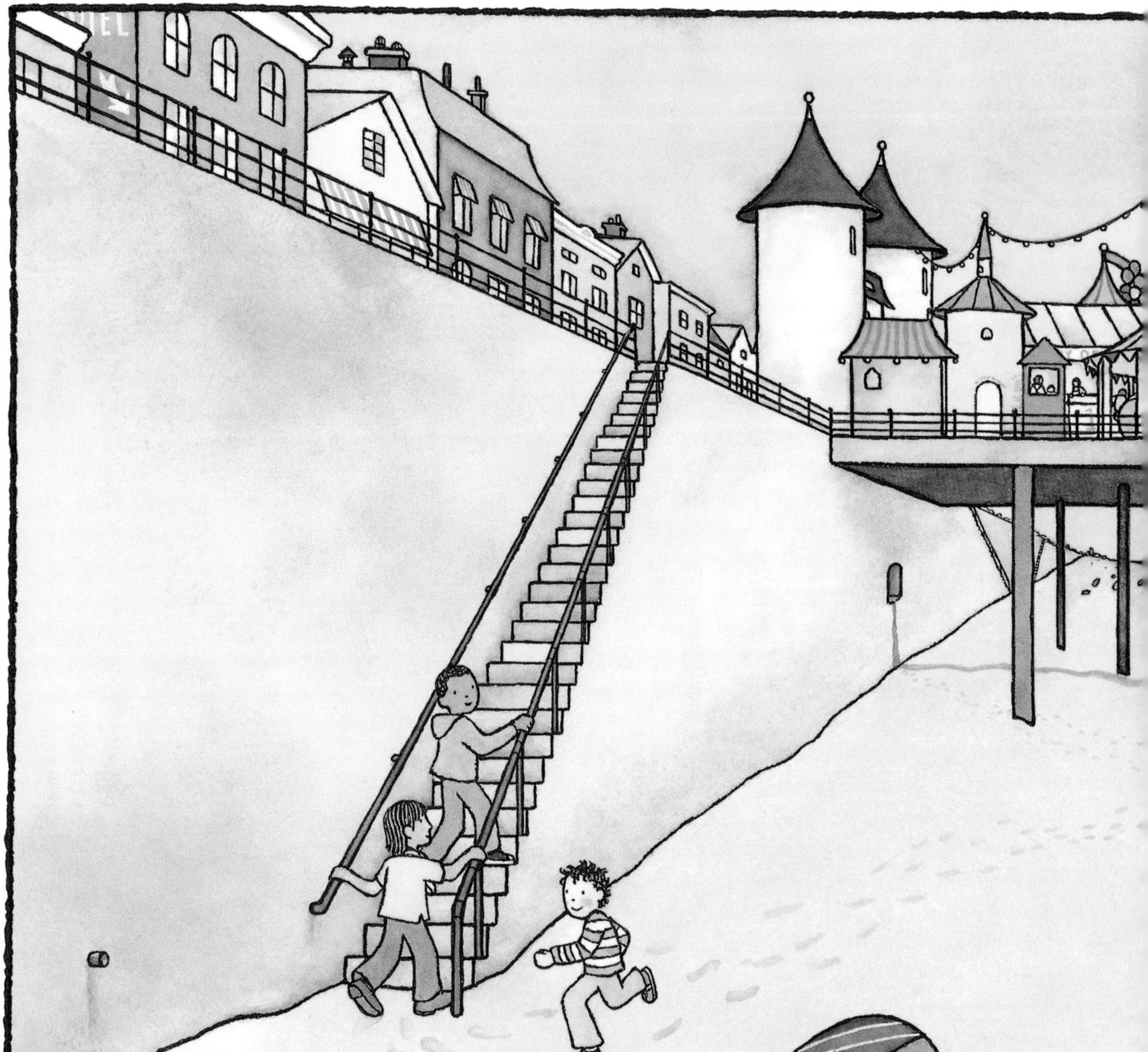

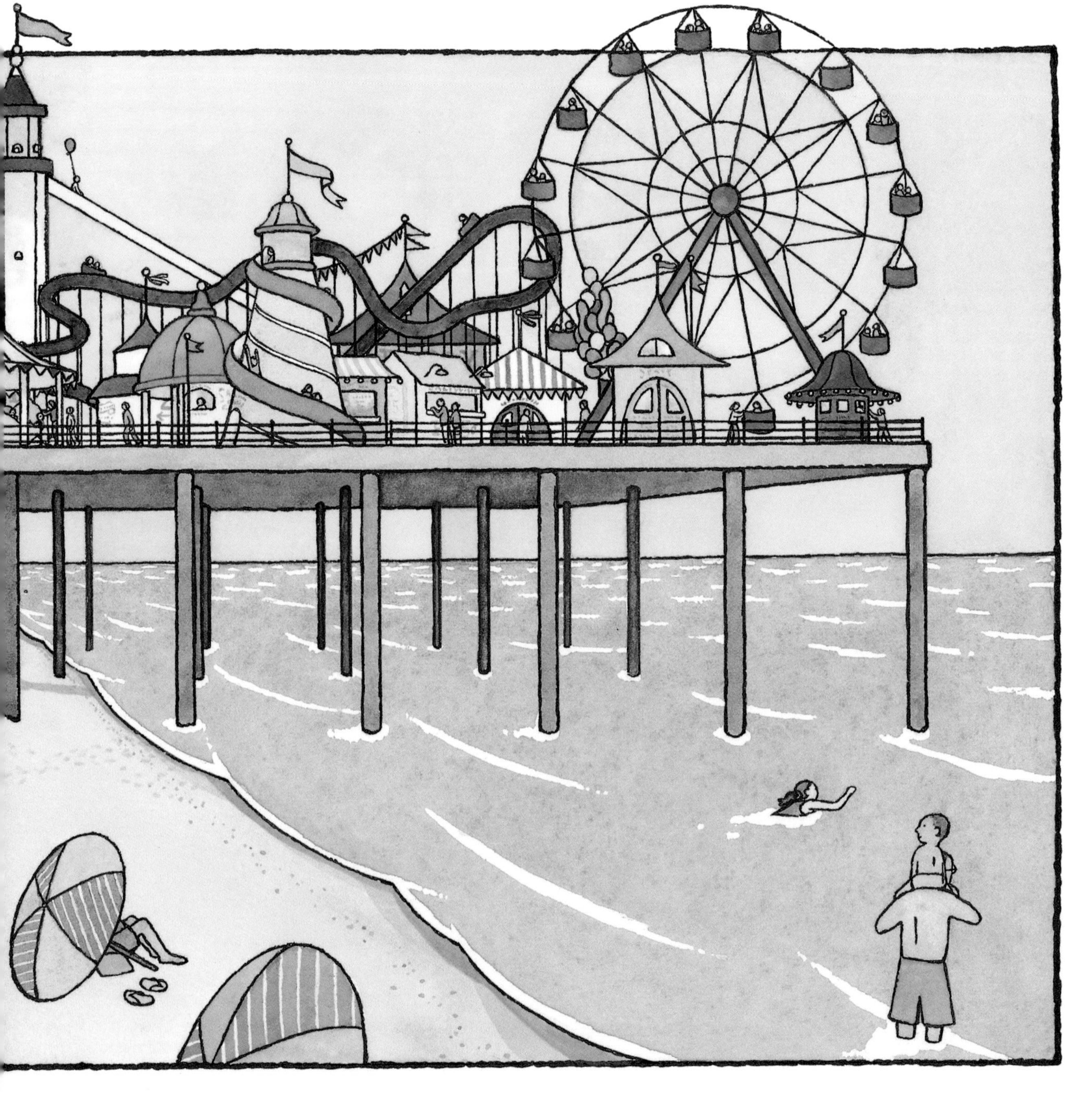

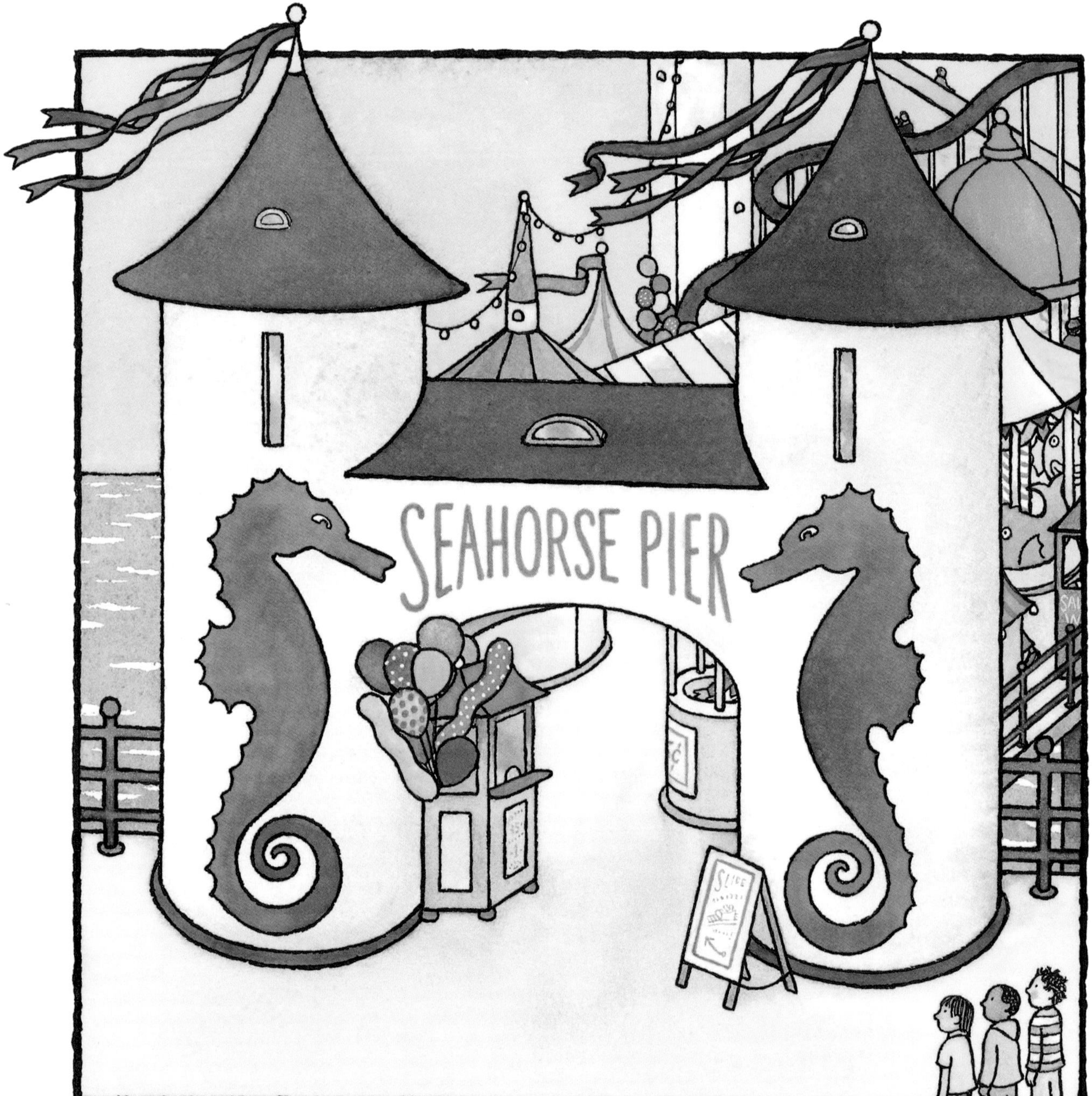
SEAHORSE PIER

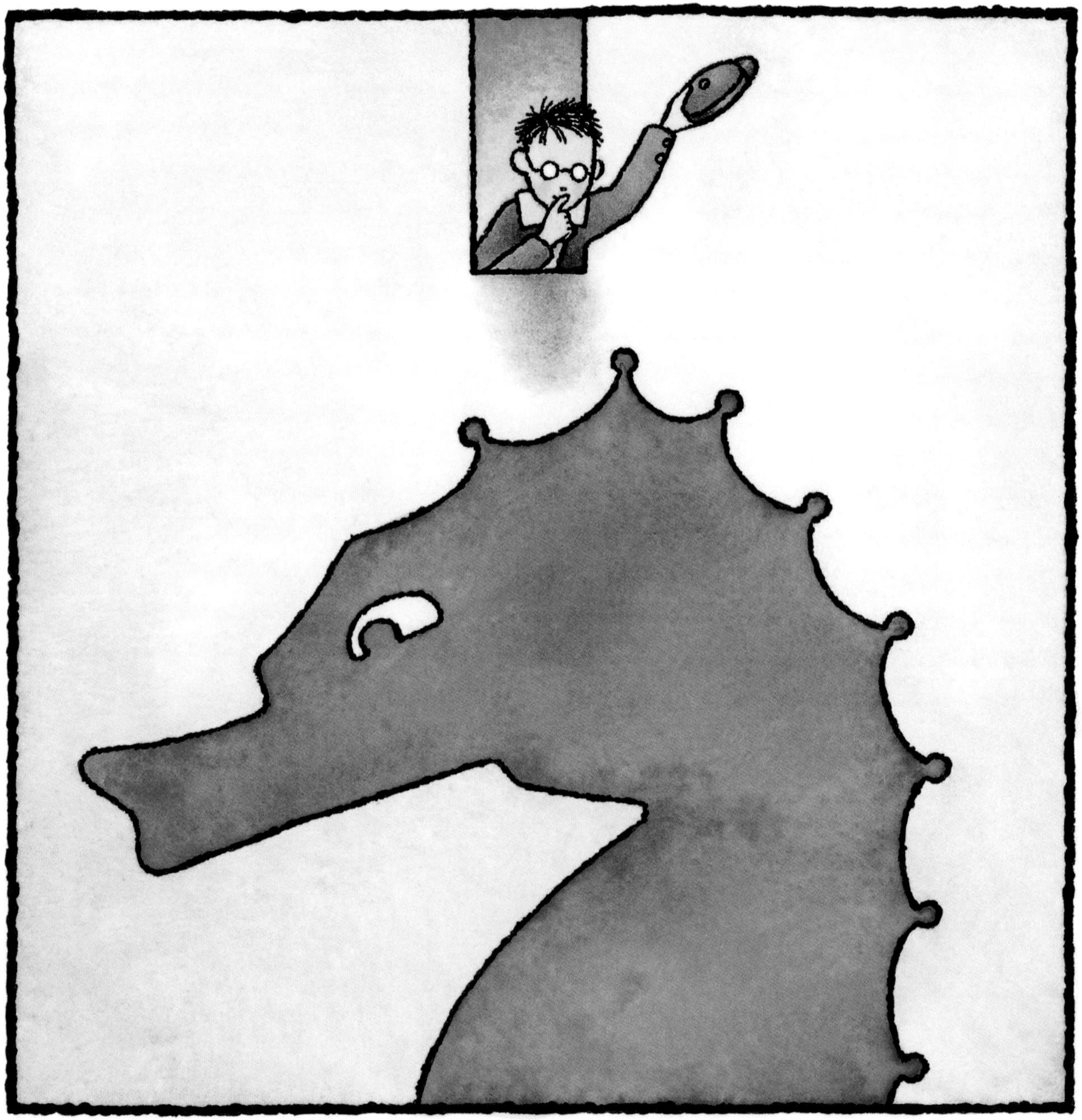

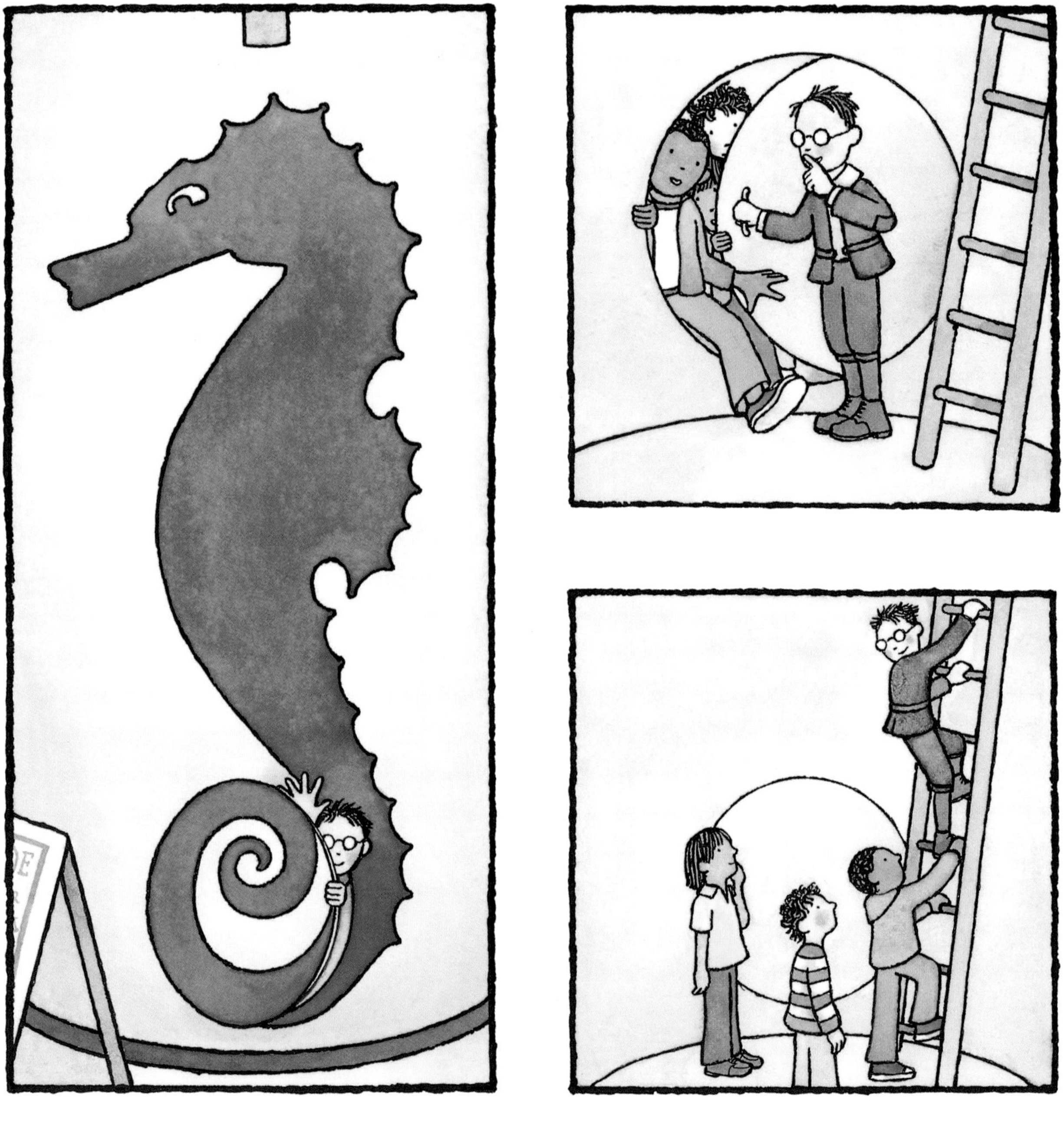

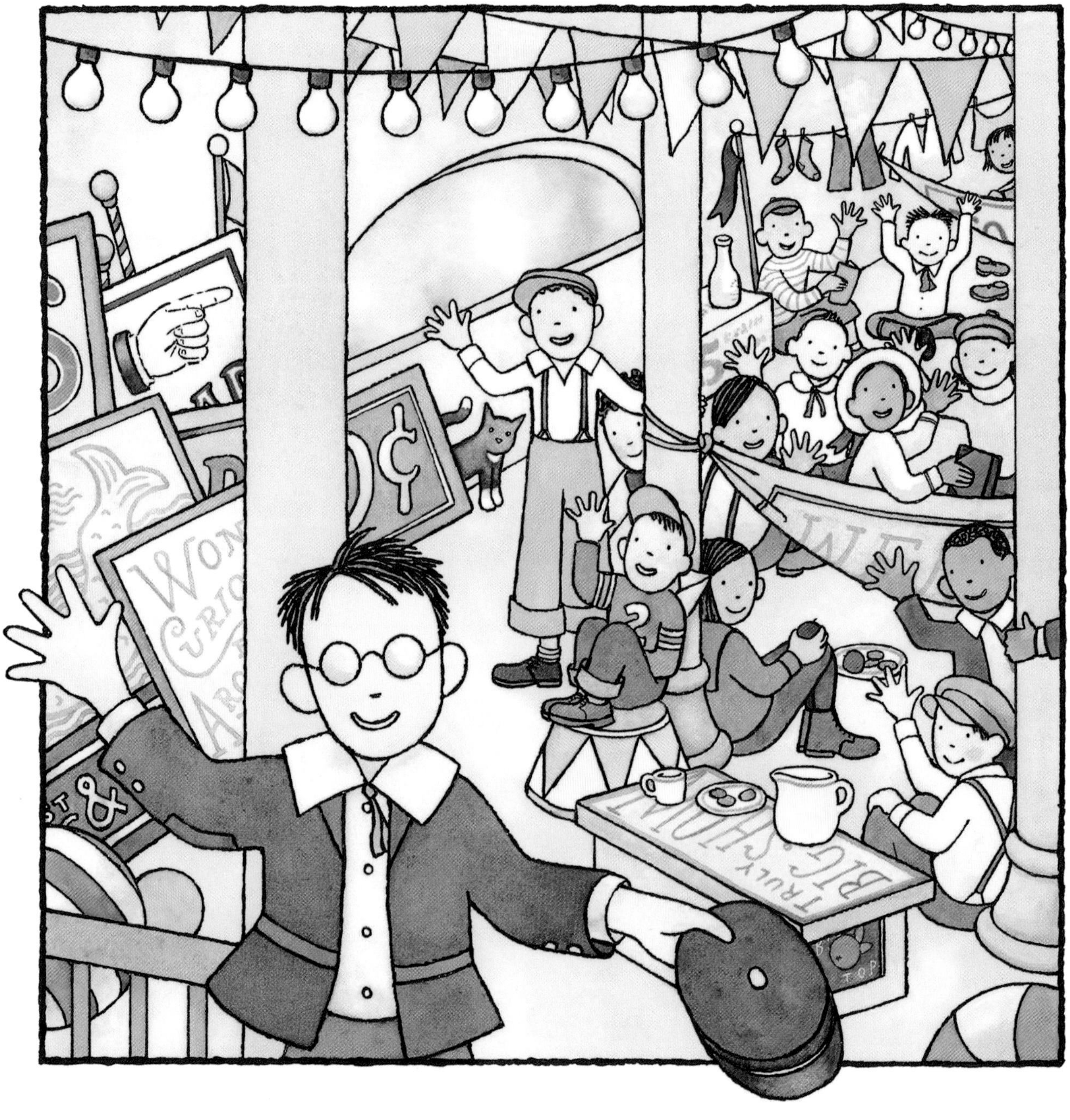
TRULY BIG SHOW!

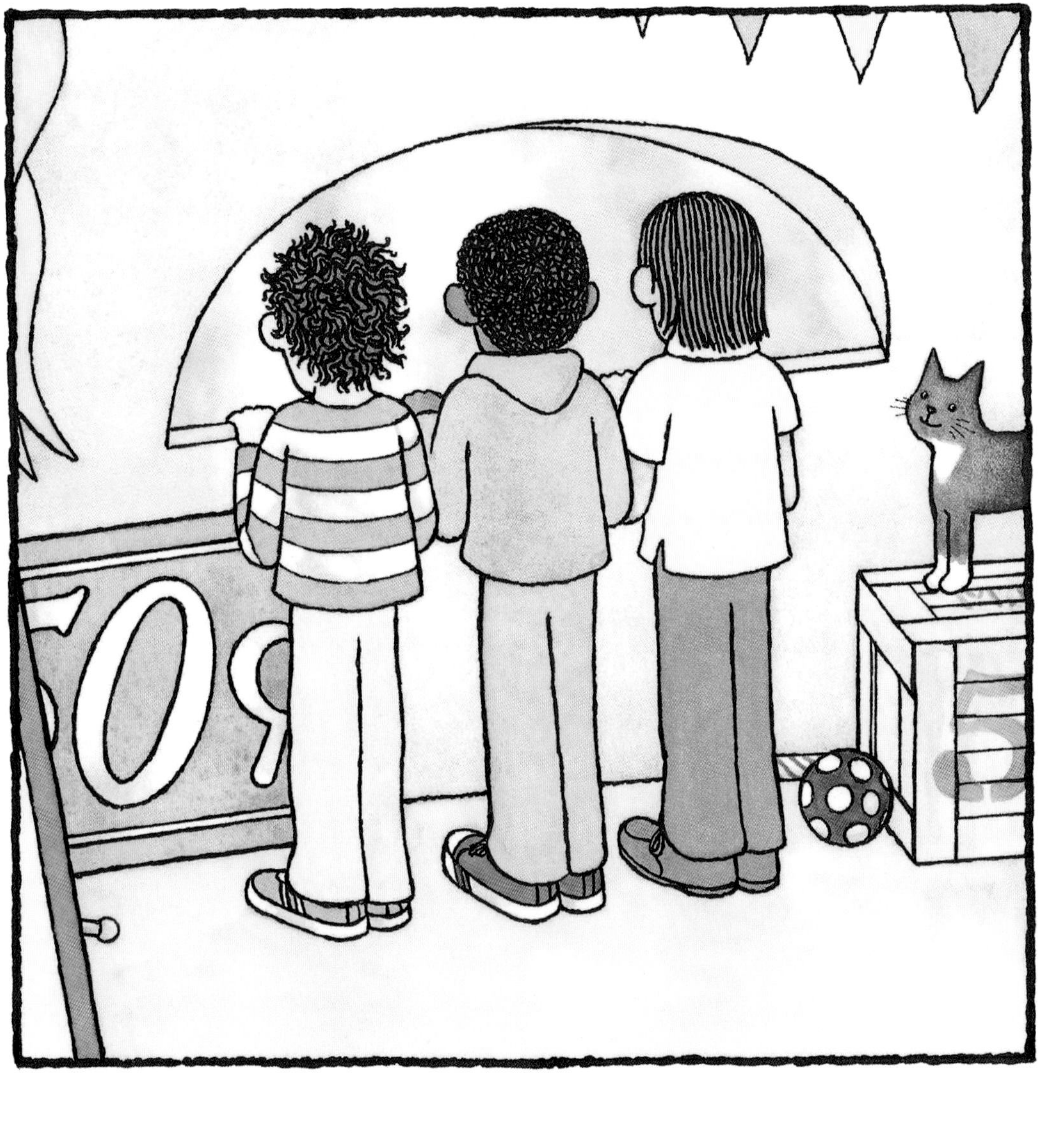

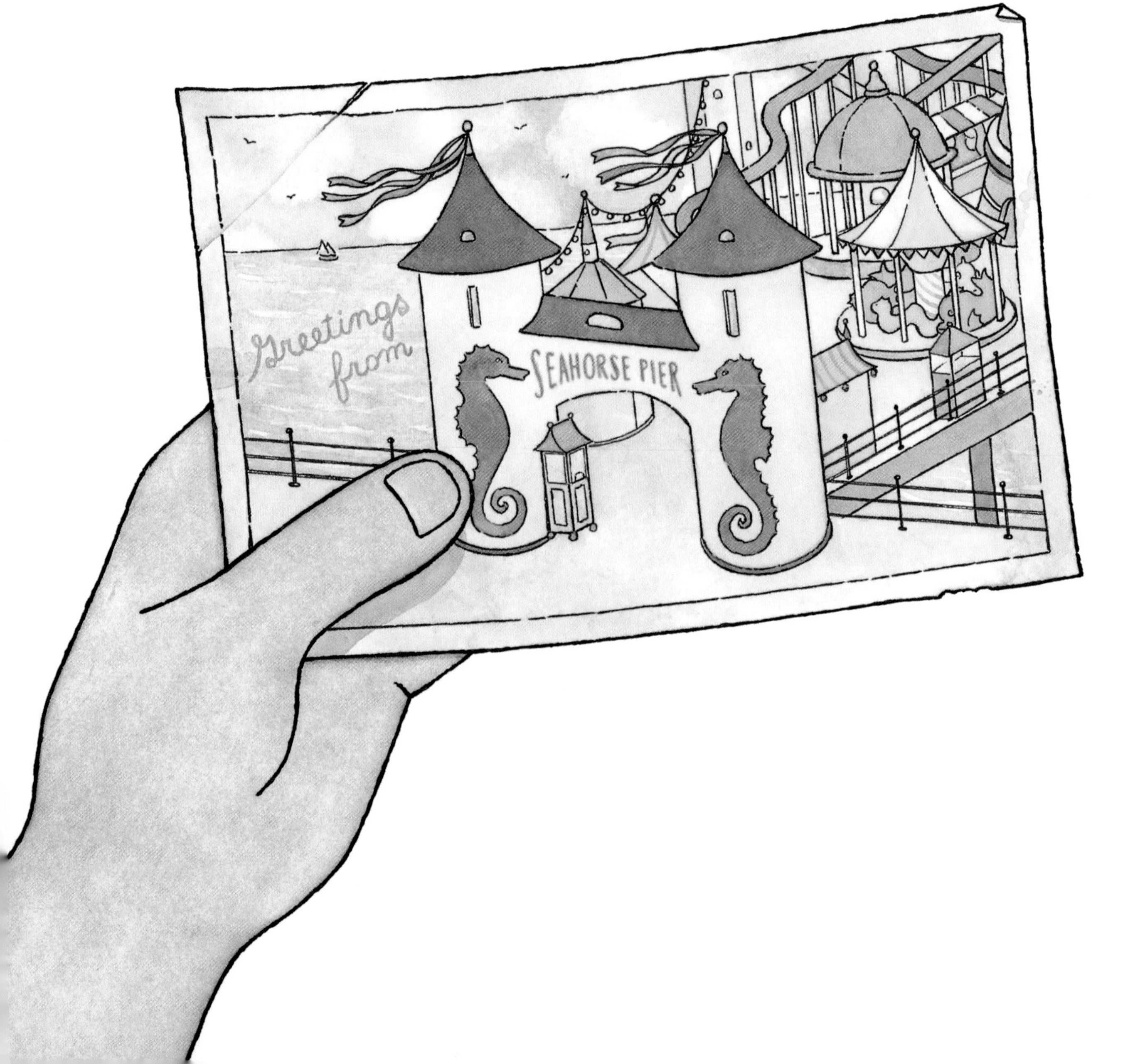

Greetings from
SEAHORSE PIER

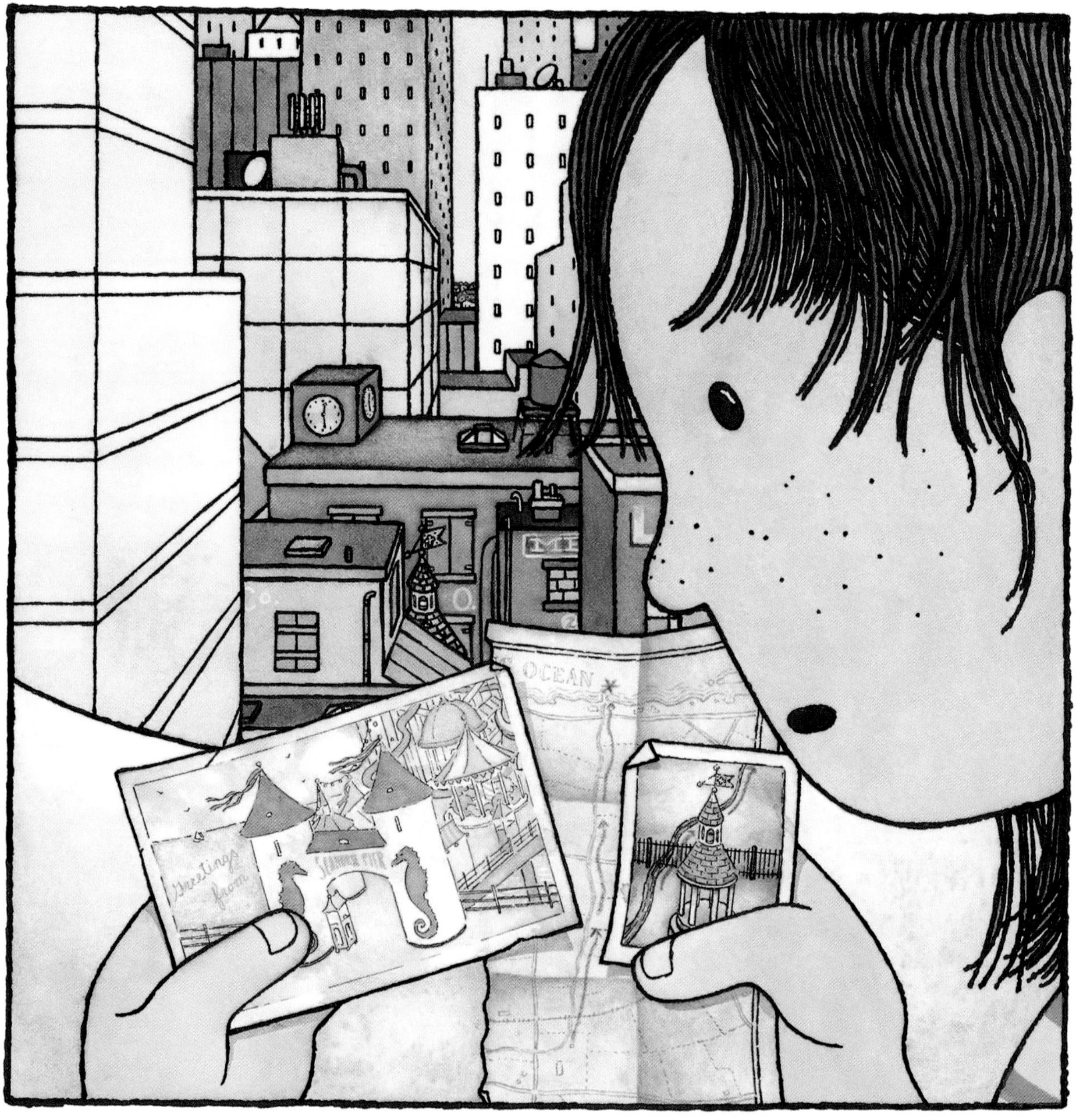
OCEAN
Greetings from

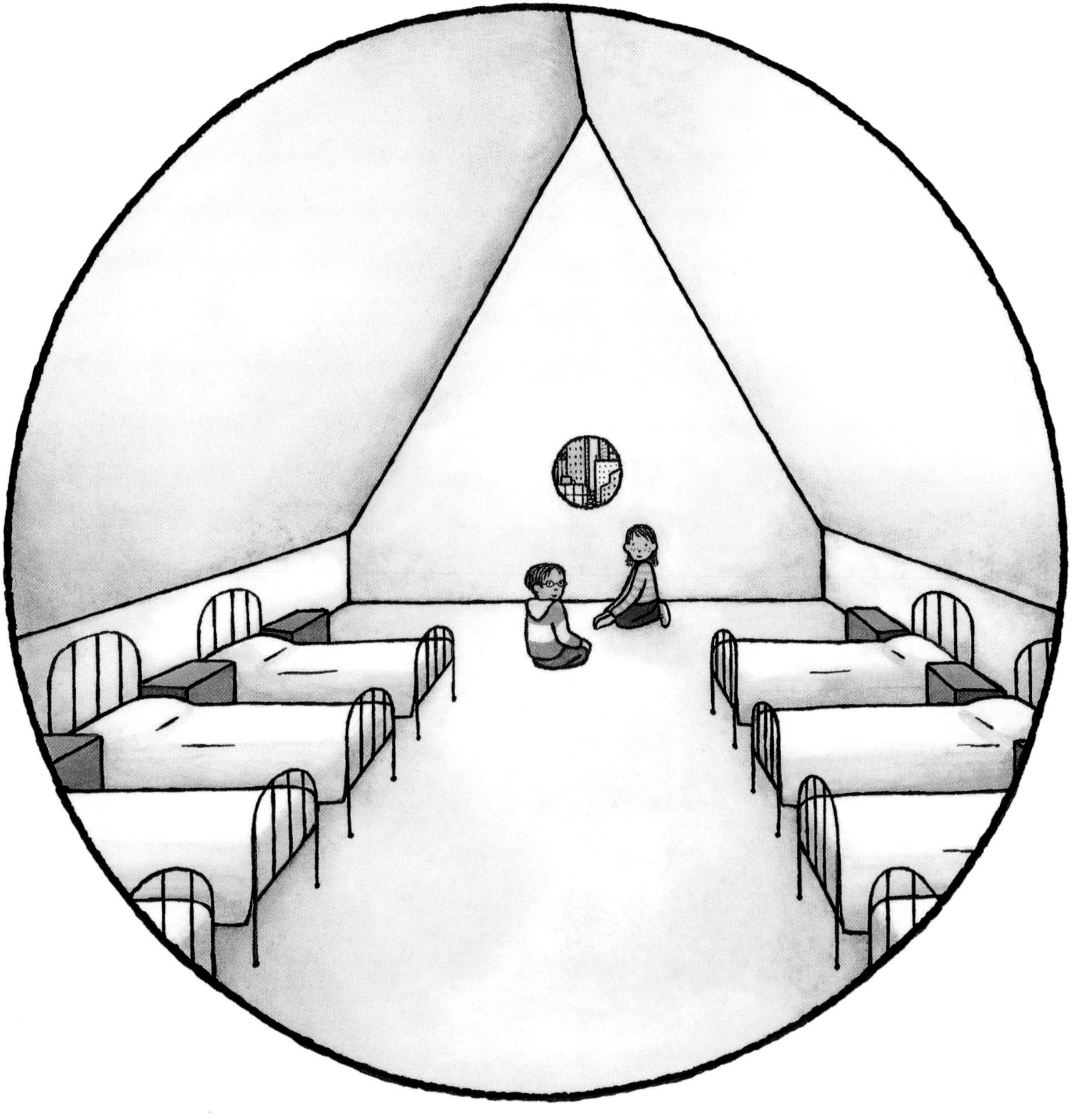

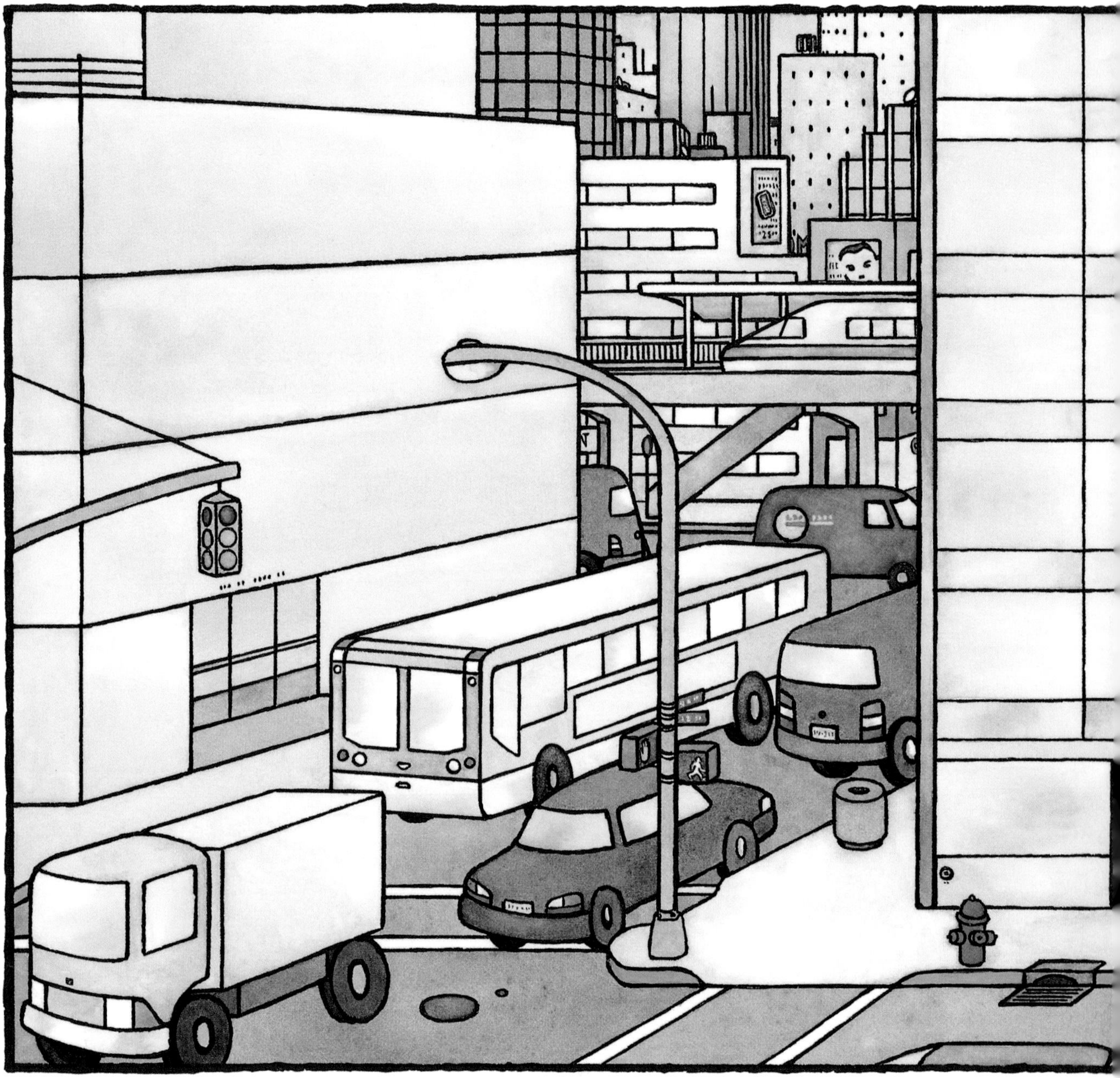

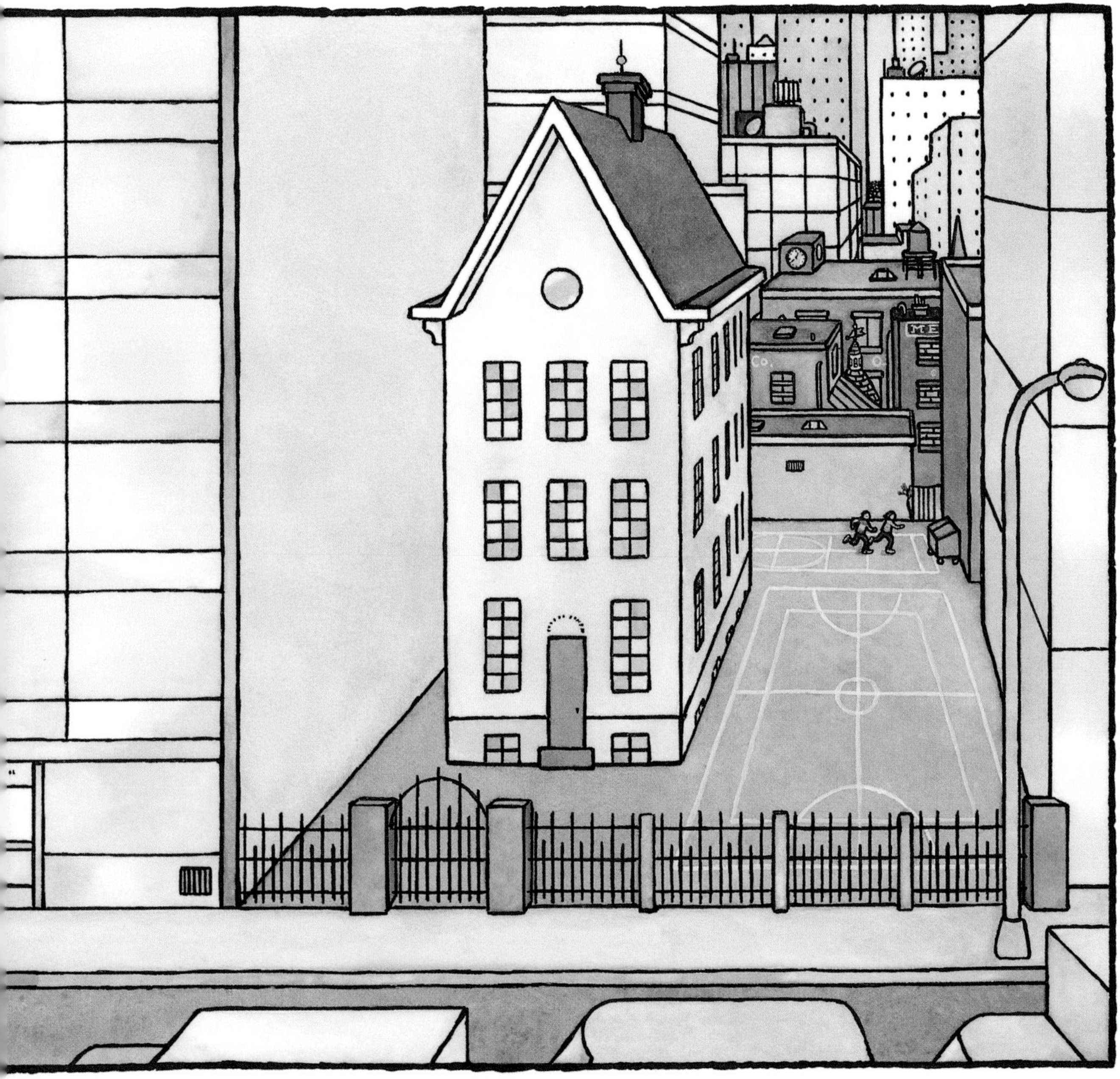

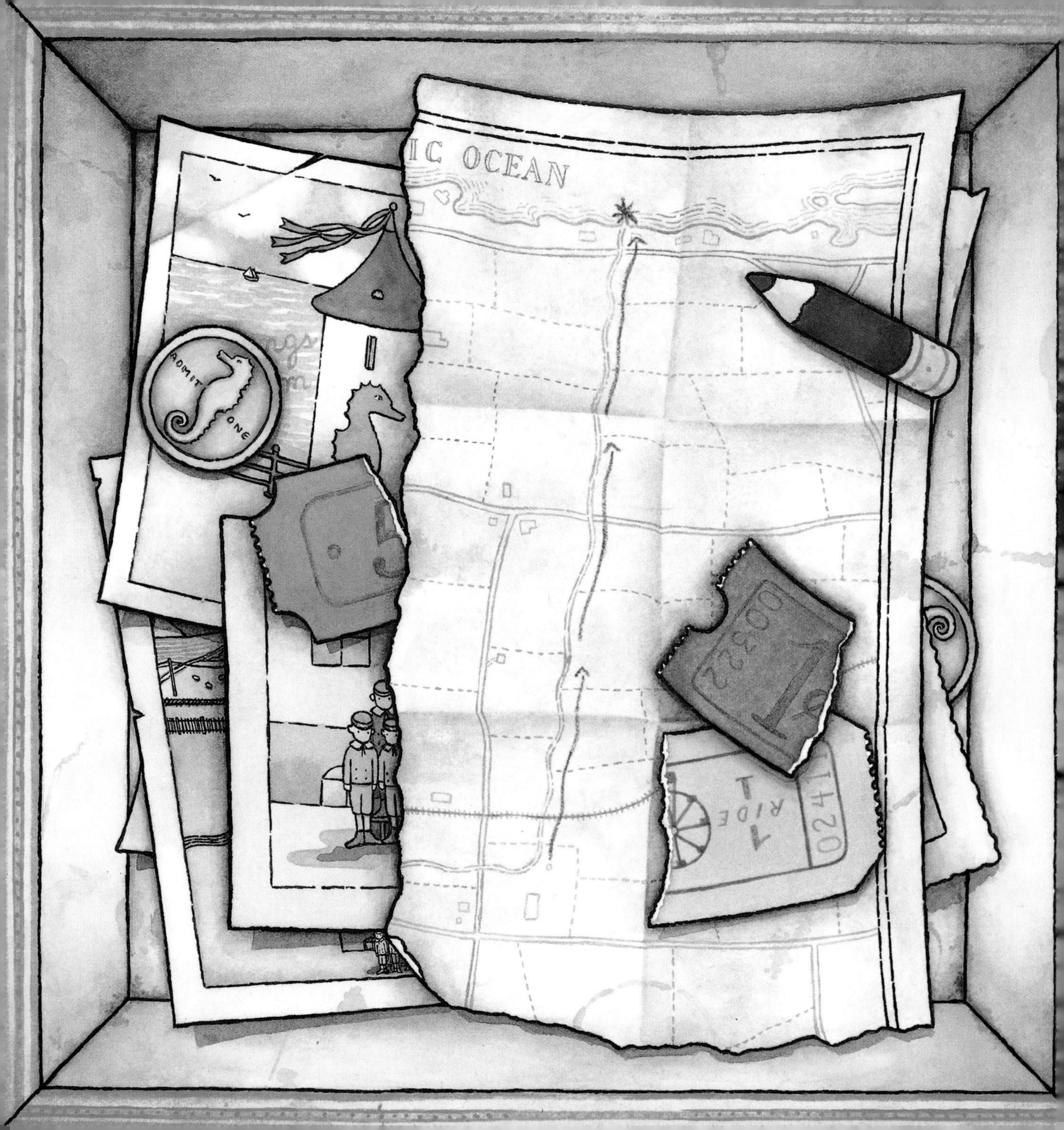
IC OCEAN
ADMIT ONE